Angels Unawares

Dedication & Acknowledgements

To the city of Lichfield and its people, who have made Yoshiko and me so welcome here in our new home on the other side of the world.

To my friends around the world who have continued to support me in my writing as I hop between genres, trying to find my voice.

To my fellow writers in Lichfield Writers.

To the memory of Jo and all the other "Beans" at Inknbeans Press, who kept encouraging me in my fantasies.

And to my family, who continue to fill their bookshelves with my scribblings.

Contents

"Do not neglect to show hospitality to strangers, for thereby some have entertained angels unawares."

Hebrews 13:2

What Readers Have Said About *Angels Unawares*

"…a story that seemed primed to be about religion and gave it a science fiction twist, somehow without allowing the latter to cheapen or override the former. It could have easily seemed incredible (in the bad sense), but rather felt rewarding."

Sarah Sisk

"… it isn't the type of story that I normally read … as I get older, my focus seems to narrow more and more on just the classic mysteries. This was a good breath of fresh air.

"… I was thinking this was going to be something like The Name of the Rose *– but it wasn't. Again, I was surprised when I figured out how it was going. "*

David Marcum, author of *The Papers of Sherlock Holmes*

"I enjoyed this, though it's not really up my alley - it's an inventive hybrid."

Al Basile, singer–songwriter, poet and cornetist whose blues CDs have been called "the most literate blues releases ever."

"Hugh Ashton is well known for his mastery of Victorian detection through his previous Sherlock Holmes stories but this departure from that genre does not disappoint. Set in Europe and the Middle East during the Renaissance, his use of language is apposite, easy to read with the flow and form of language appropriate to the characters portrayed.

"It is a genuinely human story, a blend of humanity and humility contrasted with undertones of absolute corruption. All this combined with a nod to powers that appear heavenly to those in the story and are there for the reader to discover. A very enjoyable read."

Richard G.

"Loved the book. I always enjoy fiction set in this time period, and this one held me riveted and I've been thinking about it since I finished it. Kudos to Mr. Ashton for stepping out of the world of Sherlockian London into 15th Century Italy to bring us a tale of wonder."

Veronica J. Prior

Angels Unawares

Hugh Ashton

ISBN-10: 1-912605-11-2
ISBN-13: 978-1-912605-11-8

Published by j-views Publishing, 2018

This is a work of fiction. Names, characters, places, brands, media, and incidents are either the product of the author's imagination or are fictional representations of the same.

Body set in 12pt Bembo, titles and headings in Eskapade Fraktur

www.j-views.biz
www.HughAshtonBooks.info
publish@j-views.biz

j-views Publishing, 26 Lombard St, Lichfield, UK, WS13 6DR

Angels Unawares

by

Hugh Ashton

Author of the Deed Box and Dispatch-box
series of Sherlock Holmes Adventures

j-views Publishing, Lichfield, England

Preface

Though this is set in a vaguely historical location, that of Italy in the late Middle Ages/Early Renaissance, it should not be taken as a historical novel.

Any serious students of the age will no doubt be able to discover many anachronisms and inaccuracies, for which I make no apology. This should be read as a fantasy set in our own world, rather than as a detailed description of a past age, and to that end, the names of the two principal locations echo the name of Samuel Butler's fictitious community. For the same reason, there are no temporal markers allowing the action to be placed precisely in time.

However, I hope that you will find the characters recognisable, and with luck, as credible in our age as they are in their own.

One more thing – readers often confuse the views of characters with those of the author. Robertson Davies put it well in one of his books, when a character says "George Bernard Shaw says in Saint Joan that...". He is corrected by another character who points out that Shaw makes a character express this opinion, which is not necessarily the same as that of Shaw. In this case, I believe that Davies was expressing his own opinion through the mouth of one of his characters while talking about another writer. But to cut a long story short, if you don't like the narrator's religious beliefs or moral stances, you shouldn't automatically assume that they're mine.

Illustrations are mainly Dürer – public domain. I put them in because I like them, and they're almost in the period (if not the geographical region) of the story.

Lichfield, 2017

Part 1 - Revelations

chapter 1 (Lamakan)

It has been many months, verging on many years now, since the events I write of here transpired.

I swore to myself that I would never tell a soul about them, but here, living unknown as I am in this far-off land, I feel free to commit my memories to paper, safe in the knowledge that any casual reader who is an inhabitant of this city will be unable to recognise those persons and places I describe.

And when I have finished, what then? Will I read through the pages of my notes, reopen the old wounds, and then, with a sigh of relief, consign my writing to the flames, hoping against all hope that my memories will likewise disappear as the words turn to ashes in the grate? Or will I seal them in a box, buried deep in the garden underneath the persimmon tree, for future generations to discover? Or perhaps, if I am feeling playful, I will wrap my work in brown paper, seal the package, and address it to my old friend and adversary, Signor Pietro del Murano.

But since you are reading this, you know which of these options I have chosen. I cannot have burned it, and Pietro would never have allowed it to escape his hands, if I carry out my intention of writing down the full story of his crimes, which has so far escaped the notice of historians.

It may be that in a hundred years or more there will be further evidence of what he has done, and the man often seen now as the saviour of the city may well be reviled in history books as a traitor or a monster. But who knows what the future will bring? Only you, my reader, know my future, and the future of these words I write now.

The muezzin calls – I almost, but not quite, face Mecca and prostrate myself in prayer. My servants, good Muslims that they are, are already doing so. I believe they see me as a good infidel. I speak no ill of the Prophet (peace be upon him!), but on the contrary, have come to respect him and his teachings, and proclaim as much to those who will listen. The local imam, whose Latin is at least as good as my own (learned, he told me once, from a visiting Dominican who was making his way through here to Cathay), regards me as being a lost child, but one who will find his way home in the end.

Without kneeling, I repeat, my lips moving soundlessly, the eternal prayer: "In the name of God, the Merciful and the Compassionate..." Strange words to be uttered, you may say, by one whose mouth daily spoke the words "Hoc ist enim corpus meum". And yet not so strange as if I were to venture further to the East, where men believe in a bewildering variety of deities, with a multitude of strange shapes, clusters of limbs, and heads of oliphaunts. Or those who believe in the sanctity of nothingness, and believe our lives are to be lived time and time again until we attain a pure state of not-being. At least, this is what I have been told, but I have yet to meet any followers of this strange cult.

Needless to say, the concept of the Trinity seems equally bizarre and blasphemous to many Muslims. I have attempted to explain it several times to Ali and Fatima, but they remain unconvinced by my explanations. The Imam, on the other hand, seems to comprehend the idea of the Three-in-One in an intellectual fashion, but shakes his head sadly when he explains that he cannot admit the worship of God in such a manner.

And so here I am, sitting, a glass of sherbet by my elbow, in the shade of a date palm, dressed in a style that few would recognise at home, rambling on as older men will, remembering those things which would best be forgotten, if truth be told.

☪

Let us begin with my departure from the Republic. To be precise, let us begin the day before then.

I was sitting at the table breaking my fast after Mass, when Marco burst into the room without knocking.

"Forgive me, Reverence," he stammered. "The Prefect's men are here, asking for you. They told me to tell you— request you," he corrected himself, "to attend the Prefect immediately."

"And what would Pietro want with me at this time of the day?" I asked, more to myself than to Marco. "Give them some wine and tell them I will be with them directly."

He left, and I re-applied myself to my breakfast, only to be interrupted two or three mouthfuls later by the door bursting open to admit three of the Prefectural Guards. I recognised the sergeant in charge – indeed, I had only the week before baptised his youngest child.

"Signor Fabio." I rose and greeted him. "May I offer you and your men a cup of wine? The weather would seem to demand it." Indeed, for men such as Fabio, there was no kind of weather that did not demand a cup of wine, either to cool, to warm, to keep out the damp, or to refresh on a dry day. On this occasion, however, he shook his head.

"I thank you kindly for the offer, Your Reverence. I fear I must decline, since His Magnificence has demanded your presence immediately. If we were to bring you before him with wine on our breath, I dare not think how long we would retain our present positions. There is nothing personal about this with me or with them," he added, jerking his thumb backwards at the bravos who stood behind him. "Indeed, there is no-one in the Republic whom I would arrest more unwillingly than Your Reverence, but as you know, what His Magnificence wishes..."

"...Pietro gets." I finished his sentence for him.

"Indeed so."

"Allow me to put on my cloak, if you would. I suppose you have no idea why I am being sent for?"

"None whatsoever, Your Reverence. I merely carry out His Magnificence's wishes. He does not confide in me."

"And neither would you wish him to, believe me, my friend," I told him as I fastened my cloak about me. "It is all too often far too dangerous to know too many things."

We left the house, after I had informed Marco where we were bound, and walked through the streets in silence. Though the Prefectural Guards were not an uncommon sight in the Citadel, and neither was I, the sight of us together seemed to raise a few eyebrows. Automatically, I made the sign of the Cross, and blessed many of those who stopped to gawp at our little procession. Fabio coughed.

"Pardon me, Your Reverence, but I must request you in the name of His Magnificence not to do that. The less attention that we attract, the better."

The better for whom? I asked myself, but did not speak my thoughts out loud.

We arrived at the Western Gate, where the sentry recognised Fabio and brought up his pike to salute him. Then he saw me and bowed his head, obviously expecting my blessing.

"You can bless him, Your Reverence," Fabio chuckled. "Eduardo is in need of it as are few men." The young sentry blushed at this, but I ignored this, and Fabio's gibe, and gave him the requested spiritual comfort.

"Orders came from the Presence Chamber," Eduardo told Fabio. "He is to wait downstairs." He gave this last word a peculiar emphasis, which meant nothing to me, but obviously meant something to my guards. Fabio started.

"You're sure of that?" he asked. "You've been known to make a right bloody pig's ear of things in the past, young Eduardo. Sorry about the language, Your Reverence," he added, turning to me, "but this one has been known to make mistakes sometimes."

"More than sometimes," chuckled the smaller of my guards. "That time with the chickens—"

"How was I to know?" Eduardo shouted indignantly.

"Stow it, you mob," Fabio's voice cracked like a whip. "I'm sorry for this, Your Reverence. This is none of my doing, I assure you."

"I believe you," I told him.

We marched across the courtyard, to a small door that I had never noticed before, or if I had, I had forgotten I had ever done so. It was unlocked. "Follow me," Fabio requested. It was not quite an order. "And take care. The steps are uneven and slippery." Despite Eduardo's words earlier, I was expecting to go up to the Presence Chamber, thinking this to be a private secret route, but I was mistaken. The steps led down, to an airless and windowless vault.

"There's no-one else down here at the moment," Fabio told me, his form by now almost invisible in the near-darkness. "And if I have anything to do with it, there won't be. You can have the place to yourself. And a lot better off you'll be, given some of the riffraff who find themselves here from time to time."

I began to feel alarmed. "Have you any idea at all how long I will be down here?"

"The longest I've ever known anyone be here was three months. After that they took him to Santa Lucia," referring to the convent where lunatics were kept.

I shuddered. "You don't think that will be my fate, do you?"

In the gloom, I could just make out his head shaking in denial. "You're too well-known for that, Your Reverence. I'll make sure that you're missed. A few words in the taverns, quiet-like, just saying 'we haven't seen His Reverence lately, have we?' That sort of thing. We'll all do that, won't we, lads?" addressing the other two. "Then His Magnificence will hear that people are asking after you. He'll have to let you out soon enough."

"Thank you, friend Fabio." I smiled, though I knew it was meaningless in the darkness. "Here, take this." I pulled off one of my rings, and held it out to him. "It's my ring. Take it to my house, show it to Marco, tell him to look after you all."

I felt Fabio's large rough hand take the token from me. "Thank you, Your Reverence. I'll return this to you when you're out of here. And now we must take our leave of you."

"Go with God, my sons," I told them. "And I bear you no malice for what you have done today."

I heard their footsteps clank up the steps, and the sound of the door slamming, with the key turning in the lock. At that time, almost all light faded, save for a small glimmer of indistinct light. It was impossible to tell what was its source, or, indeed how far away from me it was. I examined, as best I could, my current situation. Clapping my hands and listening to the echoes, I came to the conclusion that I was in a room of approximately the same dimensions as my bedchamber. I extended my hands before me, and walked slowly across what felt like rough paving towards the dim light.

I had gone but five faltering steps before my fingers touched the cold damp wall of my cell (for such it was), and I was able to discover that the light came from a small chimney-like aperture some distance above my head. I could make out no sky or any details, other than the dimly perceived stonework of the chimney itself. I stood there, pondering my fate. Now that I was able to take stock of my situation, senses other than my sight started to come to life. The smell of ancient piss and shit stung my nostrils. I realised that I would soon have to add to this, and the prospect filled me with loathing and dismay.

Then I heard a scuffling and squeaking around me, which I recognised as those of rats, or at least mice. I am not one of those who leaps at the sight or sound of small animals, but I did not relish the thought of sharing my cell with these beasts, which are known to be the harbingers of the plague and other maladies. I could only pray that Fabio and his myrmidons could work their magic in the taverns, forcing Pietro to release me soon.

In the distance, I could make out the sound of the clock striking the hour. Ten strokes. So soon? And yet, it seemed that I had passed days in this hole already. What a strange thing this thing we call Time is, to be sure. We make of it what we will, and yet it masters us and guides us relentlessly.

I repeated a Pater Noster, almost mechanically, and then fell into a more specific pattern of prayer, praying, not for deliverance from my confinement, but for wisdom and understanding. It was clear to me that, if Pietro were to demand my presence, I would need these qualities. Unlike Fabio, I had a shrewd suspicion of why I had been brought to this place.

As time passed, my bladder began to make its presence felt. I used my nose to locate the worst of the stink of shit, and made my way cautiously to what I believed to be that corner before lifting my cassock and relieving myself.

I returned to my glimmer of light, in time to hear the Duomo clock strike eleven. I dared not sit, as I had no idea what was on the floor below me, though my legs were aching. I had no idea how long I waited in a dazed and semi-conscious state. From time to time, I heard the clock strike, but my mind seemed incapable of counting the strokes. Hunger and thirst began to become apparent, then urgent, and I was starting to wonder if I was to be forgotten, like the poor unfortunate who finished his days in Santa Lucia, when I discerned the sound of the door at the top of the stairs being unlocked, and the hinges creaking. There was a little light, and I heard the sound of footsteps descending.

"I told you we'd be back, Your Reverence." Fabio's rough voice came as that of an angel to my ears. "Has no-one been to give you food or drink?"

"No-one," I croaked, amazed that I could still speak.

"Bastards. Saving your pardon, Your Reverence. Are we going to need to clean you up before we take you to His Magnificence?"

"A chair to sit. And... and a close-stool."

"We can manage that." Hands grasped my elbows, one on each side, firmly but gently. "Easy does it. Let's go upstairs, Your Reverence."

"What time is it?" I gasped.

"The sun's just gone down. Guess that He doesn't want you to be seen in the daylight."

There was still a little light in the western sky as we moved across the courtyard, but even the evening dusk was dazzling to my eyes, almost entirely deprived as they had been of light for the past few hours.

Fabio and the guards fussed and tutted over me as I sank into a chair. My screaming legs blessed the relief. Somehow, my cloak and cassock had become stained, and one of the guards busied himself with a wet cloth to remove the mould and slime.

"If you take these off, Your Reverence," he told me, "I can clean them much better, and you can use the time while I'm doing that to use the privy over there in the corner."

I adopted his suggestion, with a great sense of relief. When I came out, Fabio handed me a mug of small ale, and half a loaf of bread with a lump of cheese.

"Not exactly fine living, Your Reverence, but you will need something in your stomach, and I don't think you're ready for wine right now."

"I am not," I agreed, and sipped and chewed. "You're a good man, Signor Fabio."

He shrugged. "It's hard, but I try."

"As do we all. God bless you. All of you." A thought struck me. "Won't Pietro be waiting for me?"

Fabio chuckled. "We're meant to bring you before him when the cathedral strikes nine. I just decided that we should bring you out a little before then. I think we have another thirty minutes or so before you meet His Magnificence."

I closed my eyes, and prepared myself for the mental jousting that I knew awaited me. Physically, I was probably in no danger of execution – legally, that is. I was too well-known and too popular for that. Pietro would have a riot on his hands if he condemned me to death in a court of law.

But there were other ways to dispose of me, as I knew all too well. There had been too many deaths that appeared accidental. Deaths which ultimately only benefited one person – Pietro. And even if my life were to be spared, there were other ways in which that life could be made uncomfortable for me.

Fabio broke in on my thoughts. "I forgot this. Pardon, Your Reverence." He started to hand back the ring I had given him to take to Marco, and I waved it away.

"Keep it. I owe you – all of you – a debt of gratitude. In the event that I find myself unable to repay you properly," (I noticed them exchange knowing glances at these words) "I give you this ring as a poor substitute. You should be able to raise a few ducats at the jeweller's with it."

"It's too much, Your Reverence," one of them said to me. "What will you do if you give it away?"

"'What shall it profit a man if he gain the whole world, and lose his own soul?'" I quoted to them. "I have other rings." I fell to thinking how these words applied to Pietro. A man who had gained, if not the whole world, at least a large part of the world that we knew, but whose soul was, I believed, lost to him.

✠

chapter 3 (Lamakan)

Ali has just appeared in a state of great excitement. He tells me that another foreigner has been sighted in the city.

"With blue eyes and golden hair," he tells me. "He speaks a little of our language, but not as much or as well as you do, master." Flattery has always been one of Ali's virtues – or should that be one of his vices? Having flattered and been flattered myself on so many occasions, I can no longer tell whether it is a course of action to be recommended or avoided.

"Where has he come from?" I ask.

"A long distance. Several moons' march," he says. The people of this city soak up the culture of other lands like sponges, though few of them have ever ventured outside the city walls. Accordingly, though many of them can look at a piece of pottery and instantly tell you in which city in Cathay it was created, they have no more idea of the location of Cathay than they do of the islands of the Moon.

"Where is he staying?" I enquire.

"The Inn of the Thousand Stars," Ali tells me. "Will you visit him?"

"Maybe." But in truth, why should I? The likelihood that he comes from a country with whose language and customs I am familiar is a remote one. And even assuming that we can speak Latin to each other, what will we have to say to each other? I am content here, as God slowly turns to Allah, and Jesus to Isa, and Mohammed (peace be upon him!) is the Messenger.

There are few enough foreigners who stay in these parts. Those who are already Moslem are welcome enough, but the people of this city, though ready to take from others, are sometimes less than ready to give back in the form of hospitality. Oh, they are polite and courteous enough, and follow all the teachings of the Prophet (peace be upon him!) with regard to the entertaining of foreigners, but there is a certain warmth lacking in their smiles of welcome.

For those infidels like myself, the Caliph (may he live for ever!) is merciful enough in that we are not immediately put to death, as I have heard is the case in other cities. We are permitted to dwell in the city, and to pay a tax for the privilege of doing so. Only moderate pressure is placed on us to convert to the way of Islam. I compare it to the cities in Europe I have known where Moslems were unknown, other than as emissaries from exotic foreign lands, and any Jews were forced to renounce their religion and be baptised, on pain of death. Here, there is a thriving village of Jews in the heart of the Old City, with a synagogue to which my friend Isaac sometimes leads me on their Sabbath. My week ends with three days on occasion, therefore, with Friday being a visit to the mosque to hear my friend the Imam's sermon (only half-understood by me, I am afraid, as my Arabic is improving only slowly), Saturday being spent with Isaac in the observance of Shabbat, and on Sundays I celebrate Mass, often for myself, but sometimes for the few Christians (none of them followers of Rome, alas) who are resident here.

Truly, I am coming to realise that God is greater than anything I was taught to believe as a young seminary student. But more of that anon…

☪

chapter 4 (Nessuna)

I must have dozed off in the middle of my musings, as the next thing I knew was Fabio tapping me on the shoulder.

"Wake up, Your Reverence. It is nearly nine o'clock. It won't do to be late for His Magnificence, will it?"

"Indeed it won't. Thank you for all you have done."

He shrugged. "It is little enough. Please pray for us poor sinners."

"And you for me, my friends. I am ready. Let us go."

We walked across the courtyard. I sniffed the air and could smell burning, though the evening hardly seemed cool enough for a fire to have been lit. Through the twilight, I could make out black shreds dancing in the breeze, and wondered what they were. We mounted the Great Stairs that lead to the Presence Chamber (I write that "they lead", but verily, I have no way of knowing whether they are still in existence, or whether the Citadel, or indeed the city itself, still stands. Maybe the stranger of whom Ali told me will know, but I have my doubts).

As we passed through the doorway, the clock began to strike, and I smiled to myself. Pietro would not be able to accuse me of being late, at any rate, no matter what other charges he might see fit to bring against me.

The Prefect was seated behind the Table of State, a jug of wine and some beakers before him. The half-stripped carcass of a roast chicken lay on a platter, pushed to one side. Pietro put his head on one side, and addressed Fabio. "Has the prisoner behaved himself?"

"Admirably well, Your Magnificence," Fabio told him.

"I am a prisoner?" I asked Pietro. I tried to look him in the eye, but he looked away.

"I would have thought that your lodgings today would have informed a man of your perception of your status," he replied, still avoiding my gaze.

"May I be permitted to know on what charge I have been arrested?"

"Who said you had been arrested?" A lazy smile, which I knew all too well from the past, came to his lips. "You are a prisoner. That is a fact. All else is lawyers' talk. Dust in the wind." He toyed with the beaker in his hands, and addressed Fabio. "Leave us," he ordered. "I will call you when you are needed again."

"As Your Magnificence wishes," answered my guard, and Pietro del Murano and I were left alone in the large echoing Presence Chamber.

"Sit," he told me, gesturing to a chair facing him. I sat. "Wine?" reaching for the jug and another beaker.

I shook my head. "Thank you, no."

"Frightened I'll poison you?"

"No, Pietro, not that." My use of his name seemed to produce a change in him, and he slumped back in his chair, his pose of authority gone.

"Gerardo, why did you do it?" There was more sadness than anger in his voice.

"Do what?" I played for time.

Now there was a little anger showing. "Write it all down, you fool! It was bad enough that I knew that you knew, but when word came to me that you had been recording it all, I had to act. There was no way I could allow you to keep on doing it."

I allowed my face to register enlightenment. "You mean my diary?"

"Is that what you want to call it? A scurrilous collection of lies and half-truths, defaming me, and accusing me of infamous crimes against man and God and nature."

"Lies, Pietro? Half-truths?" Again, the use of his name produced a change.

"Maybe not complete fiction." He shrugged. "But the point is, these things should never have been written down. What if an enemy were to read what you had written? What," and here he leaned forward, a new edge in his voice, "if you were that enemy, and wished to use these things? Or if you were to show them to our neighbours, the Duke or the Count, with a view to taking my place once they had successfully disposed of me?"

"Your Magnificence knows that I could never entertain such thoughts."

He laughed bitterly. "Maybe I believe Your Reverence, but do I believe little Gerardo?"

"You may safely do so." I could contain my curiosity no longer. "How did you discover?"

"My eyes and ears in your household."

The truth suddenly dawned on me. "Marco?"

He nodded. "It was a simple matter of a few ducats to persuade him to serve two masters. While you were enjoying yourself down there," he gestured with his thumb towards the floor, "my man was admitted to your lodgings by Marco, who led him to the recess under your study floor. He brought the papers to me unread."

"Fabio?" I was shocked once more.

"No, I know Fabio has a high regard for you. I used Christoforos, who is unable to read Latin, as you know."

I shuddered. Christoforos had entered Pietro's employ in an unspecified capacity some ten years previously. He was rumoured to be of Greek extraction, but no-one appeared to be certain of this. Some had marked him down as Pietro's private torturer, but there was no proof of that, as there was also no proof that he acted as the unofficial executioner of those who had incurred the Prefect's displeasure. Tall and thin, his dark figure flitted through the rooms of the Citadel like a sinister shadow. If addressed in Latin, he betrayed no sign of comprehension. He and Pietro conversed in the vernacular, or, when the matter was one that the Prefect wished to remain secret, they conversed in a tongue that appeared to be understood by those two alone.

"I know he does not speak the language, so I am guessing he does not read it either. I have never seen him with his nose in a book, at any rate." I laughed, in an attempt to lighten the mood.

Pietro laughed too, but there was little humour in it. "I agree, the spectacle of Christoforos reading a book would be a strange and wondrous sight. However," and he returned to seriousness, "I do read. And what I have read this evening gave me little pleasure."

"So?" I was understandably anxious to know what might befall me.

"First, let me congratulate me on your writing style. I found myself quite gripped by your accounts of my actions, though I knew the plot well, and what would transpire next."

I bowed my head. "Thank you."

"However, you need not flatter yourself that your words will be preserved for posterity." He nodded toward the stove that stood in one corner of the room. I recalled the smell of burning that I had noticed earlier, and the black shards dancing in the moonlight. "I see you understand. Good. So that is the words disposed of. But what to do with the author?" He stood and smiled the smile of a cat regarding a mouse. "I would be sad to have to put you away. We have been friends, of a kind, for a long time, have we not?"

Part II - Genesis

chapter 5 (Nessuna)

Indeed we had been friends for a long time. We came from similar backgrounds – indeed, as children, our families lived in adjoining streets.

My father was a shoemaker, his a draper. Our mothers used to draw water from the same well on the corner. I would like to imagine that we played together as young children, but my childhood memories have faded to the point where I can no longer remember the faces and names of my companions at that time.

My first recollection of Pietro as a distinct individual was at the seminary where we were both being taught by the Dominicans. We must both have been seven or eight years old, but as I say, my memories of those days are hazy. I already knew my letters, my father having painstakingly taught them to me, and I was able to string them together to create simple words. We each had a burned stick and a piece of wood on which we were meant to write our letters, after which we would scrape off the writing with a knife, and start afresh.

I and the boy sitting next to me exchanged whispered messages when Fra Romeo was otherwise engaged. We had already established each other's names.

"Can you read?" Pietro whispered to me.

"A little," I whispered back.

He scribbled with his stick for a while, and held out his wooden board for my inspection. "Read that."

"F - A - R - T," I read quietly. "Fart!" I pronounced proudly.

My triumphant exclamation coincided with one of those times when the world seems to have stopped and everything is at peace. There was a burst of giggling from the boys immediately round us, together of whispers of "What did he say?" "What?", followed by even more laughter.

Fra Romeo strode up, habit swaying. "Gerardo, isn't it? Stand up, boy! Did you say what I thought I heard?"

"I don't know what you thought you heard, Brother," I replied. I wasn't trying to be clever or cheeky. I was genuinely trying to discover what he thought he had heard, but it earned me a clip round the ear.

"Why did you say that word?" he demanded.

"I was reading, Brother."

He frowned. Another clip around the other ear. "And where would you see that word to be able to read it?"

"Off his board, Brother." I pointed to Pietro.

"Ah, I remember his name. Pietro, yes? Show me."

Pietro held up his board, on which he had attempted to erase the offending letters, but they were still clearly visible.

Another clip on the head, but this time it was Pietro, not me, who received the blow. "Why did you let him," pointing at me, "write that on your board?"

"It was me who wrote it, Brother," Pietro confessed.

"So you two can both read and write at least simple words?"

"A little, Brother," I said.

"Me, too," said Pietro.

"I want you two to sit at the front, but not next to each other - change places with those two," he told us. "I want you where I can keep an eye on you, and where I can help you best with your studies."

Blessed Fra Romeo. And blessed Pietro. If he had never written that word, and I had never read it out loud, then the fact of our being more advanced in our letters than the rest of the class would never have come to light. And Fra Romeo, though he had a hot temper (as we frequently discovered), had a genuine love of teaching and helping boys to achieve their best. Sadly, this was not true of all the brothers.

chapter 6 (Nessuna)

Pietro and I continued as friends through the school. Fra Romeo proved to be our strongest ally in our struggle to succeed. I subsequently discovered that all the brothers, and the Prior himself, viewed us as "precious jewels to be treasured" (many years later I discovered these very words in a letter written by the Prior to the Archbishop). It seemed we were marked for greatness, and in hindsight, this seems to have been the case, with Pietro assuming the Prefecture, and I rising to my position in the Church.

Both of us had fine boy soprano voices, and sang in the choir of the brothers' church. The love of music has stayed with me all my life, but unfortunately, my adult singing voice, though adequate enough for the performance of my priestly duties, is of no real quality. That of Pietro, on the other hand, developed into a fine tenor, and he continued to sing at gatherings, and for his own pleasure, but unfortunately did not sing in the church choir.

We were, however, marked for other things. If you were to see me now, you would laugh, but I was a singularly attractive young boy, as was Pietro. It is well known that unfortunately the monastic life can attract those who prey on young children, and Fra Anselmo was one of these. He made little secret of his attraction to me as he guided my studies. At times, I could even feel his stiff member through his habit, as he pressed against me. I mentioned this to Pietro, who seemed more worldly-wise about these things, as we sat one evening by the piazza, idly throwing stones at the passing dogs.

"He does it to me, too," Pietro said.

"And what do you do? It makes me go all funny inside. I don't know what to do," I confessed.

"I move away. He doesn't like it, but he knows he'll get in trouble if we tell the Prior what he's up to."

"Someone said the Prior was like that, too."

Pietro laughed. "How could he be? He's really old. He must be fifty years old at least."

"Sixty," I said.

"Seventy," countered Pietro.

"A hundred and thirty," I said, and we both burst out laughing.

Pietro shied a stone at a mongrel, and missed. "It's not really something to laugh at," he said. "We should do something."

This was the first I learned of Pietro's natural skill in plans and trickery as he unfolded his idea to me.

A few days after this conversation, Fra Anselmo asked me to stay behind after the others had left, telling me that he wanted to go through a chapter of Boethius with me. As Pietro passed me, he winked, and I nodded in return.

As expected, Fra Anselmo leaned over behind me, pressing his body against mine. This time, rather than freezing in place, which was my normal practice, or moving away, which was Pietro's, I moved back, pressing myself against him in my turn. I could feel him moving rhythmically against me, and then he suddenly pulled away and stopped.

"Turn round, young Gerardo, and face me," he commanded.

I did so, to discover that he had opened his habit, and displayed himself to me. I was terrified. Though I had seen my father naked on a number of occasions, I had never seen his member in the erect stiff state that Fra Anselmo was now presenting. It appeared to be pointing straight at me like some kind of terrible weapon.

"Take it," he commanded, pointing down at himself. "Take it, and put it in your mouth." I hesitated, and out of the corner of my eye, I could see the door slowly opening a crack. I reached out my hand, and grasped blindly. Immediately my head was forced down by Fra Anselmo's hand, and my lips were about to touch the hideous object, when I heard Pietro's voice.

"What are you doing, Anselmo?" he shouted.

The effect was immediate. My head was released, and Fra Anselmo stepped back hurriedly, re-fastening his habit. I sat back in relief, wiping my hands on my tunic, and thanking the Lord that I had not touched Fra Anselmo with my lips.

"What are you doing, you little tyke?" he growled.

"Observing. Learning. As you teach us to do," said Pietro, calmly. "And you tell us that we should bring the light of knowledge to those who remain in ignorance, do you not?" He stood still, a half-smile on his lips, as Anselmo digested the meaning of his words.

"What do you want?" The friar was now obviously shaken. "I have no money, as you know."

"Are you accusing me of blackmail?" Pietro stood, calmly confident, his arms akimbo, and his head thrown back.

"I don't know." Fra Anselmo almost wailed these words, clearly frightened of the young boy who stood before him.

"Then let me tell you what's going to happen," Pietro, now firmly in control of the situation, told him. "You will first apologise to Gerardo here, and to me, for the harm you have done us by your attentions to us."

With a bad grace, Fra Anselmo began his stammering apology.

"It would go better if you were to kneel before us," Pietro told him.

Grumbling, Anselmo dropped to his knees and repeated the words that Pietro instructed him to say.

"That's better," said Pietro when this was over. "No, don't get up." It was amazing to see this friar, in the peak of his life, being ordered around by a young boy, almost as if he were the pupil, and Pietro the master. Later, when I came to know Pietro better, such a situation seemed normal, but I was then witnessing Pietro's extraordinary control of others for the first time, and I watched entranced. "You will desist from all such behaviour in the future," Pietro told the now weeping friar. "Not just with us, but with all boys here. Is that understood?" Anselmo nodded. "Nor will you attempt to take any kind of revenge on Gerardo here or myself by penalising our studies. I am not asking you to favour us, you understand, but simply that you treat us and our work fairly." Another nod. "And lastly... you will confess the sins that you have committed in the past, and confessed just now to the Prior."

"I cannot!" exclaimed our teacher. "He would dismiss me from the Order."

"If you are truly penitent, I am sure that God and the Prior will forgive you. Now go, and sin no more." He waved his hand in dismissal, a gesture I was to see him use so often in the future.

Fra Anselmo slunk off. When he was out of sight, Pietro threw his arms around me and kissed me full on the lips. "We did it!" he exclaimed.

To my surprise, and his, rather than shrinking away, as I had done with the friar, I moved into his embrace and returned the kiss.

"Do you want to– you know?" he asked me.

"Do what?"

"Do what he wanted to do with you? We could take it in turns," he suggested. "First me, and then you."

So we did, having first taken ourselves to a more private place where we removed our clothing. I must confess that it was an enjoyable experience, but since we had both to reach puberty, the enjoyment, at least in my case, lay more in the fact of our doing something forbidden than it did in any physical pleasure.

"Was that a sin?" I asked when it was all over.

"I don't think so," he said, but somewhat unconvincingly. "Anyway, I'm not going to mention it in confession. If it is a sin, and I don't think it is, it's such a small one, because we're friends, isn't it?"

"Perhaps," I said, but I was far from believing it myself. In any case, I did confess it to my priest (not to one of the brothers, I can assure you), and he told me it was a most grievous sin against the Holy Ghost, and gave me a stiff penance.

Of course, telling a child that something is wrong only serves to make it more attractive in his eyes. And so when Pietro suggested that we continue, we repeated the experiment a few more times in the coming weeks, but the novelty of wickedness soon palls and we both soon tired of the game (for verily, it was no more than that to me, at least).

I suppose that this is the time to tell you that this was the only such experience in my life. I have never again been attracted by male flesh, and though I have been sorely tempted in my time by some of the girls and women I have met in my life, I have maintained my vows of chastity. Perhaps you may think this a little old-fashioned, but when so many of my sacerdotal colleagues are seen to behave in inappropriate ways, I feel it incumbent upon myself to disassociate myself from their way of life.

As for Pietro, it seemed that for him, carnal relations served two purposes: firstly, for physical release. He once told me in a moment of confidentiality, that he had never experienced a nocturnal emission (would that I had been spared that embarrassment in my life!), and that therefore relations with another person were a necessity for him. Secondly, he used such relations, with men and with women, to advance his path in society, to the pinnacle that he eventually attained.

And Fra Anselmo? He kept his word for two years, and then he vanished without warning. One day he was with us, and the next day he was gone. The brothers whispered that his bed had not been slept in, and that none of his possessions, save the habit he had been wearing, was missing. Even his missal was in its place beside his bed.

A search of the city and the area around discovered nothing, but about six months later, a report came from a village in the hills that a shepherd had followed one of his sheep into a cave, where he had discovered the desiccated and emaciated body of a man, clad in a Dominican habit. From the scanty description provided, the body could have been of no-one other than Fra Anselmo.

I confess to feeling some guilt in the matter, feeling that we had in some way driven the poor man to take his life, but Pietro, on the other hand, was jubilant, and saw it as a triumph of his will over another's. I observed this and, while I still loved Pietro as a friend, I saw him as someone to be treated with caution, even at that tender age.

chapter 7 (Lamakan)

Fatima has just interrupted my writing to let me know that my friend Isaac is here.

"Lead him to me, Fatima," I tell him.

Isaac joins me beneath the date palm, and Fatima and Ali bring almonds and sherbet.

"Shalom, my friend," I say to him.

"And may God's peace be with you," he answers me.

We sit together, sipping our sherbet and nibbling the almonds. We sit in near silence, exchanging occasional pleasantries about the song of the birds in the trees, the sweetness of the sherbet, and the taste of the nuts. Life is indeed good here.

"And to what do I owe the pleasure of your company, friend Isaac?" I ask him, when a suitably polite time has elapsed.

He turns to me, his face animated. "Angels, the messengers of God, are here among us," he says.

Usually, Isaac is one of the most sober-minded of my acquaintances. And though of course I believe in the existence of angels, I do not believe they manifest themselves to elderly Jews living in a city dedicated to the memory of Mohammed (peace be upon him!).

"You are sure?" I ask, though I know full well what the answer will be.

"I am sure," he tells me. "I saw the young man with my own eyes.

He had golden hair and bright blue eyes. He was very tall, slender, and his gaze was like a flame. His garments were of pure silver as he walked through the market."

Ali had failed to tell me all. Or perhaps he never knew these details that Isaac has just given to me. In any case, neither Isaac nor Ali realises the full significance of what they are reporting to me.

I shiver, and Isaac notices.

"You are cold?" he asks, solicitously.

I tell him the truth. "I am afraid," I say.

"'The fear of the Lord of hosts is the beginning of wisdom,' as you know," he reminds me. "To have a fear and to be awed by His messengers is nothing to be ashamed of. You and I and all in this city would agree with that."

I smile at him, but I am still afraid, and it is a fear I cannot share with anyone.

Isaac and I discuss angels from the standpoint of our respective faiths, and from that of our hosts' faith. Isaac adds what he has heard of a belief in divine messengers held by those who live far to the east, beyond the Indus River. At most times, I would relish such a conversation, but the knowledge that such a one as Isaac and Ali have described is in the city is disturbing. If I am honest with myself, it is terrifying.

☪

chapter 8 (Nessuna)

Returning to my youth. Pietro and I were indeed ornaments of the Order. We were fortunate, I suppose, in that we lived in a city which had declared itself a Republic, governed by a Prefect, rather than a hereditary Duke or Count or Prince.

In theory, a man from any rank of society could become Prefect, if he had the ability (it was generally assumed that no woman could fill the post successfully), and for Pietro and myself, this certainly seemed to be true.

The brothers would often take us to attend civic events, where we were dressed in (borrowed) finery, and rubbed shoulders with the great men of the city. It was clear that the intent was to make us familiar with the way in which the city worked, and the invisible wheels which turned continually, as well as making our faces familiar to those who turned those wheels.

My father and mother were proud of what was happening, but at the same time concerned that I was stepping outside my station. "It doesn't do to stick up too far, my father told me. If I've got a nail on a shoe that's sticking up, you know what I do with it?"

"You hammer it flat?" I said. I was tired of this conversation, which we seemed to have repeated many times.

"I hammer it flat, that's right. And if it won't respond to the hammer, what then?"

"You take a pair of pliers and you cut off its head," I answered wearily.

"That's right, lad. Don't you be that nail, that's all I'm telling you."

I sighed, and went off to change into my "glad rags", as my mother called them. "You'll still talk to us when you're Prefect, won't you, son?" she kept asking me.

"I'm not going to be Prefect, Mama," I always told her. "I'm going to be an Archbishop or a Cardinal. Maybe even the Pope," I joked.

Mama crossed herself. "May Mary and all the blessed saints in heaven preserve you if you carry on talking like that."

But if the truth were told, I had no wish to join the government of the city. I found myself more and more drawn to a life in the Church. Did I have a true vocation? Was God calling me to His service? I kept asking myself. I knew of some who had entered the Church in a spirit of near-mockery, seeing it merely as a way of enriching themselves.

For myself, I had no illusions that I was able to manipulate others to my will in the way of which Pietro was capable. The way in which he had cowed Fra Anselmo so long ago had merely been a foretaste of the way in which he was now able to control almost anything and everything around him, almost without others being aware of his power.

I saw, for example, how he was regularly invited to Prefectural Council meetings – the only person, other than scribes and the Councillors themselves, to be permitted to do so. On more than one occasion I overheard Councillors discussing among themselves how they wished that an exception to the rules could be made in the case of Pietro, allowing him to be a full member of the Council before he reached the age of twenty-five.

Granted, Pietro was advanced in his studies. Like me, he was fluent in Latin, spoke fair Greek, and his knowledge of civil law was at least the equal of mine in canon law. As far as mathematics and natural philosophy were concerned, we had the best of teachers, and I am not boasting when I say that we could have disputed on equal terms with the doctors of Bologna, the Sorbonne, or Oxford.

Both of us enjoyed exercise, and by virtue of the comparative freedom of our city, aided by Pietro's talents of persuasion, we were allowed to practice our swordsmanship – which we would have been forbidden to do had we lived in one of the Duchies or Principalities. This was one area in which I excelled over Pietro, who wove complex mental webs with his sword, seeking to entrap the opponent's mind with their complexity. Unfortunately, while he was developing these long drawn-out strategies, a more direct opponent, such as myself, was able to penetrate his guard and win the bout.

It was the same with chess. If he survived the first few moves, while he was plotting his strategic gains, he invariably won, following the course he had worked out in his mind many minutes earlier, but it was all too easy for a less thoughtful player to take advantage of the time while he was laying his plans, and to take the game at an early stage.

It was inevitable, I suppose, that we should end up going our different ways.

The brothers, though they may have secretly wanted me to enter the government, and through me, to have a voice in the running of the city, as they assumed (poor fools) that they would run the city through Pietro, professed themselves delighted that I wished to enter Holy Orders. Maybe they saw it as a natural complement in the realm of spiritual power, in contrast to the temporal power that it was evident Pietro wielded with such skill.

Though I say it, I was a good priest. I may have lacked Pietro's talent for coercing others into doing my will, but I did discover that I possessed a gift for reconciliation, which allowed me to solve disputes between my parishioners in matters of business or their personal lives, to help couples with their marital problems, despite my celibate status, and to organise the church in such a way that it came to the notice of the Bishop, who visited me and recruited me to serve on his personal staff.

It was work I enjoyed, and it soon became clear that I was a man to be reckoned with in the city and the immediately surrounding area. Modesty forbids that I should speak too highly of myself and my achievements, but I can safely say that those with a problem and a disagreement would sooner bring it before me for a solution than they would before the city magistrates. In other words, I was successful in my chosen calling. Nor did I neglect the spiritual aspects of the post. I continued to study and to pray for God to aid me, and it seemed to me that my prayers were answered.

Though my stipend was nominal, I encouraged my petitioners to be generous in their donations to charity – which I interpreted liberally as meaning the support of my parents, as well as that of an orphanage outside the city walls.

And what of Pietro? As he made his way upwards through the ranks of the city government (I nearly wrote that "he drifted", but with Pietro there was no such thing as drifting – he steered a deliberate course towards his goals, and Heaven aid those who barred his way) we naturally saw less of each other, though still mutually professing friendship.

We met to dine at regular intervals, and told each other of our respective successes, occasionally admitting (on my part, anyway) to occasional failure. Naturally, our accounts displayed only those sides of ourselves that we wished to display, but a priest hears more than he speaks, and I could not help but note some of the stories I was told.

There was, for example, the story of how he had seduced the young daughter of one of the more senior Councillors, and then turned the tale on its head, making her out to be the guilty party, who had set her cap at him, and taken advantage of his youth and lack of experience of the world. Improbable as this might seem, I was told that it was believed by the Council, and Pietro was able to use this to gain the support of the very Councillor whose daughter he had seduced to gain the position of Market Inspector, in which post he had ample opportunity to feather his own nest. This was an opportunity of which he took full advantage, the story continued.

There were other such stories, most of which turned on his almost uncanny ability to persuade others to carry out his wishes, even when they went against their own interests. Before long it appeared that he would become Sub-Prefect, the deputy to the ruler of the city, even before he had reached the legal age at which he could become a Councillor.

One evening, I was returning from the Bishop's Palace, where I had been working late, and I happened to see Pietro ahead of me, walking fast towards the West Gate of the city. The hood of his cloak was pulled over his head, obscuring his face, but I could easily identify him by his gait. Usually, I would have walked a little faster to catch up with him and to exchange greetings, but for some reason I held back, and followed him at a distance, taking care to keep to the shadows where I would not be noticed.

He walked out of the city, and took the road leading to the hamlet of San Barbara, but turned off after almost half a league towards a copse of alder trees half-hidden in a hollow. I dared not follow, knowing that it was more than likely that my presence would be discovered. I had no idea what Pietro was doing, but the fact that he seemed to be taking care to disguise his identity raised my suspicions.

I returned to the gate, and asked the guards there if they had ever noticed any strangers in the vicinity of that hollow. They told me that they had not, but one mentioned some strange events that he and others had witnessed from time to time.

"One night there was a light in the sky. Not as big as the moon," he told me, "but pretty bright. It sort of moved around in the sky. You couldn't see it from down here, but you could make it out from the top of the tower up there."

"A shooting star?" I suggested, but he shook his head.

"No, sir, it wasn't one of those. I've seen enough of them to know the difference. This sort of stood still and then moved down – it sort of fell, like – in the direction of the place you're talking about. Then the light went out."

"And then?"

"The light stayed off until the end of my watch. No idea what happened next."

Another guard stepped forward and reported a similar event. They were unsure of the dates on which they had seen these strange events, but I asked them to let me know if they saw such a thing again, and even to wake me if possible, so that I could observe it for myself.

As I walked back to my house, I turned over in my mind what

manner of thing the men might have seen. The most likely explanation was that they were drunk – the Prefectural Guards had a noted liking for wine – and had been mistaken in what they were observing.

It occurred to me that maybe there had been a divine visitation – that we had been blessed by a visit by one of the saints, or maybe even an angel.

I decided that I would investigate the place at some time soon, for if indeed we had been chosen to receive a divine visitation, was it not my duty as a representative of the Church, to discover the truth of the matter?

chapter 10 (Nessuna)

I shall tell you of what I discovered when I visited the hollow I had seen my friend visit a few days previously.

It was a calm sunny morning – a perfect day for a stroll in the country, if I had nothing better to do, and since so many of the laity seem to believe that a priest is only busy on Sundays and when he is in the church, my passing through the city gates attracted no attention.

Despite the good weather, the small aspen copse presented a somewhat bleak aspect as I approached it. The small almost perfectly circular area of flat ground in front of it, some fifty yards in diameter, forming the floor of the hollow, was obviously uncultivated and ungrazed. The grass and wild flowers grew lush and thick. Strangely, though on my approach to the hollow I had been continually forced to look down to avoid putting my foot into a rabbit's hole and thereby turning my ankle, or tripping over a molehill, there were no such evidences of animal life within the circle.

As a boy, I had heard stories of faerie rings, around which the Good Folk danced before proceeding with their tricks and mischief, and within which no animal would set foot, but such rings (though I had never seen one with my own eyes) were supposed to be a mere two or three yards at most in diameter.

As I walked around the area, I became aware of one or two strange phenomena. Firstly, the grass in the centre of the circle appeared to be drier, almost parched, compared with that elsewhere. Furthermore, this dried grass was in the shape of a circle, about two yards across. Perhaps this was the faerie ring, I thought, and crossed myself, reciting a Pater Noster and an Ave. Secondly, when I had finished my prayers and looked around me, I discovered a square depression where the grass had been flattened, about five spans on a side. This could not be natural, I told myself, and continued my investigation. To my astonishment, I discovered another four such squares of flattened grass, and from what I could tell, they were evenly distributed around the circle of dried grass in the centre.

As I made these discoveries, I became slowly aware of the impression that I was being watched by someone or something that remained invisible to me. I crossed myself once more, telling myself that God would protect me, and praying for His assistance. I was by now convinced in my mind that the lights that had been seen by the guards and these strange markings of the grass were in some way connected, though I could not for the life of me form that connection. I no longer had any belief that this place and these markings were in any way connected with angels or with divine visitations. There is a certain feeling when one comes into close communion with the divine which transcends description.

What I felt at that time was not that feeling, but one which seemed to radiate malevolence and evil. To come into contact with the Devil and his works (as I have done on several occasions in my life) is a powerful experience, equal in its force to encountering the Creator, but unlike that latter, was one that could be described and related to others. I feared for Pietro's soul, if he was indeed in communication with the forces that gathered here.

As I have said, the day was a fine one, but even so, I found myself shivering as I stood in that grassy circle. I became aware that there were no birds singing, and then my eye was caught by a bright speck of light winking from the bushes in the copse. I instantly considered, and as quickly dismissed, the idea that this was the light that the guards had seen. It was clear that this was the sunlight being reflected from some object.

I made my way over to the place, and stopped to pick up a cylinder of shiny metal, about the size of my thumb. I turned it over to reveal some markings on the side, but peer at them as I might, I could make nothing of them.

They were in no system of writing that I recognised. I was, of course, familiar with Latin, Greek and Hebrew systems of writing. In Constantinople, I had seen the language of the Russ, the Georgians and the Armenians, and in Cairo that of the Arabs, of some of those living beyond the Indus, and even that of Cathay. But these resembled nothing I had seen before. They were so perfectly regular, that it was hard to believe that the hand of man could have delineated them. I cast about for more of these objects, but this was the only one that I could find.

All this while, I was conscious of the feeling that I was being watched. Feeling foolish, I lifted up my voice and called out, "Is anybody there?"

I received no answer, and truth to tell, I had expected none. The sound of a dog barking a long way off came to me, and with it, the spell seemed broken. Was I imagining things in this strange setting?

The question still remained, though. Why had Pietro come here? Had the light that the guards had seen anything to do with his visit? And what was the meaning of the strange markings and depressions in the grass? Were they in any way connected with the small cylinder that I had discovered?

As much as Pietro and I professed our friendship, I felt that this was not a matter on which I wished to question him. There was a feeling in my mind that all was not as it should be with regard to this place and Pietro's presence in it, and it was with something of a heavy heart, with an increasing sense that I was beginning to lose the friendship of one whom I had regarded as my closest companion for many years, that I started to return to the city.

When I reached home, I immediately wrote a record of what I had seen and placed it in a box which I hid beneath a loose floorboard in my study. This formed the first of the documents that Pietro burned shortly before I left the city for the last time.

✠

Part III - Acts

chapter 11 (Lamakan)

I sit beneath my date palm and think about Ali's and Isaac's angel. Does he know I am here? I ask myself. Is it now time for me to move on? Or would moving away simply draw attention to myself? Attention that I am keen should not be drawn?

I cannot believe that it is mere coincidence that he is here in the same city as me. But how would he have found me? My name is no longer what it was, and those who know me as an Italian, and not just as a foreigner, believe I am not from Tuscany in the north, but from Calabria in the south. I have been at pains to conceal my identity, and I truly believed that all traces of my former self had been erased. Even my appearance is changed – my hair, once black, is silver, and I have grown a beard which to my mind completely changes the shape of my face. I am an old man now, and the handsome straight-backed youth that I once was has gone long ago, transformed into a stooped and occasionally doddering (I admit it) old man.

Once I wrote down what I knew of Pietro and his doings, but those writings are now ashes in the wind, scattered long ago across the hills and plains of Italy. I have determined to write again. The world should know the truth, before the angel discovers me. Maybe my words will not be discovered in my lifetime, or even in the lifetimes of my (non-existent) children or grandchildren – but some time in the future. I will write in Latin, rather than one of the dozen other tongues I could choose. Our vernaculars change, even in our own lifetimes, and what I write now may be unintelligible in a hundred years. But Latin... Latin will never change, being dead as it is, and yet it is the lifeblood of the Church, and hence of civilisation.

How I bless the brothers, especially Fra Romeo, for teaching me to love the language, and be at home with it. I praise God for a clear mind, trapped as it is in a failing and ageing body.

So I will continue telling you what I know of Pietro del Murano, the Prefect of our city. It is not a continuous narrative, but a story composed of episodes. This is necessarily true, as our lives do not run as a continuously smoothly flowing river, but rather as a mountain torrent, dashing down, tumbling as a waterfall down a precipice, dawdling in pools, winding peacefully between green banks, and repeating the process many times before reaching the sea.

The narrative of my own life was interrupted many times as my calling took me away from the city on many occasions. I visited Rome and the Holy Father frequently, sometimes staying there for two or three months together. Once I spent a year in Byzantium, and three months in Cairo, and I even made a journey (which I sincerely trust will never be repeated) to England, where I passed a miserable, cold, wet six months in the city of Canterbury. At that time, I was obviously unaware of events in our city, and only learned afterwards of what had occurred through gossip and hearsay – neither of which forms a reliable basis for a historian on which to build his relation of events.

☪

chapter 12 (Nessuna)

§hortly after the episode I have just related, a painter, one Jean Vernet by name, arrived in our city from France.

Vernet (he preferred to be addressed in that way) had made his way to our city, having fled France for reasons which were never totally apparent.

Some said that he had murdered one of his lord's ministers there, others that he had murdered the lord himself. Another story was that he had fallen foul of the authorities as the result of actions similar to those of Fra Anselmo, that I wrote of earlier, and yet another that he had seduced the wife of his lord, who had borne his bastard son. Still more insisted that he himself was that bastard son, who had been banished from his father's domain in order to avoid embarrassment.

One thing was certain — Vernet was a talented painter of people, animals, and scenery. His representations of birds and beasts were such that you could imagine them wandering off the page into your life, and you almost expected the men and women that he depicted to start conversing with you.

I first met him soon after he arrived in the city. Others had been talking about him for a week or more, but I had yet to set eyes on him until he came to my room in the Bishop's Palace, and requested an interview.

Being as curious as the next man, I gladly assented, and he was shown, bowing, into my presence. I was surprised. From the stories I had heard, I was expecting a tall handsome man of commanding presence. Instead, I found myself regarding a small dark man, hardly taller than a dwarf, with a mass of untidy dirty black hair. I was tempted to dismiss all the tales of seduction that had led to his flight, but reminded myself that one of the greatest lechers of my acquaintance had a similarly unprepossessing appearance.

Vernet's clothes had obviously once been of good quality, but were old and patched. Stains of paint spattered the tunic, and there had been no discernible attempt made to remove them.

He doffed his cap and made a bow.

"How may I be of service to you?" I asked him.

"Your Serenity is in charge or commissioning work for the Duomo, I believe?" His voice was harsh, and his Latin was strangely accented.

That is not the title by which I am addressed, but I did not bother to correct him. I acknowledged the fact.

"As I walked around the Duomo, I could not help but remark – pardon me, Your Serenity – that the painting of Our Lord's Baptism was in a sad state of repair. Furthermore – and again pardon my presumption – even had it been in the state in which the painter finished it, it would have been unworthy to adorn the fine edifice in which it is displayed."

"So you wish to restore it?"

"I wish to replace it completely, with a painting of my own."

"Naturally, you will wish to be paid for this work?"

He shook his head. "I wish no payment for my work on this. However, I would welcome compensation for the materials – the boards, pigments, and tools – that I will employ."

"And how much do you estimate that bill to be for a picture of the same size as the present one?"

He named a sum which seemed high to me, and I shook my head.

"But, Your Serenity, there must be blue in the picture. The sky overhead, not to mention the Blessed Virgin's robe as she watches her Son receive his baptism from John. Gold leaf also is needed for the halos of the saints portrayed."

"I can comprehend gold being expensive, but blue?" At that time,

I knew not nearly as much about artists and their ways as I do now. Vernet proved himself to be a great source of knowledge as time went on.

"The blue, Your Serenity," Vernet continued patiently, "is to come from lapis lazuli, which is, as you are no doubt aware, to be found only in the mountains that lie beyond Persia to the east. It is rare, and must be hewn from the living rock, and then transported over many leagues, through many cities, before it reaches us. The browns and the yellows are of course local to this area."

I nodded as though this was all actually familiar to me, and I had temporarily forgotten the fact. "Very well, then. You may start on the picture. I am sure you will want some of the money in advance, though."

Of course, I was correct in this assumption – craftsmen like Vernet are as material as other men, no matter how much they may claim divine inspiration for their work. He named a sum, and I scribbled on a piece of parchment and affixed my seal.

"Take this to my treasurer, Giovanni. You will find him in the Citadel. Show the paper to the guards at the gate and they will direct you. Giovanni will give you money. Keep all orders, invoices and receipts and present them to Giovanni."

"Thank you, Your Serenity." He took the paper from my hand, and I noticed his own, paint caked in the creases.

"How long before you are finished?" I was expecting an answer of some length, perhaps six months, so I was surprised when he informed me that he would have a painting ready for my inspection and approval by the time of the next full moon – not three weeks away.

"You work fast," I told him.

"So others have said," he answered me. "I simply work at the speed which feels right to me. I simply ask that I remain undisturbed, either by you, or by anyone else, during that time "

He bowed, and took his leave.

When I first saw the finished picture in Vernet's workroom, well before the date he had named for its completion, I was amazed. I could scarcely believe that human hands had created such a thing. The poses and expressions of the principal characters: the Baptist, Our Lady, and Our Lord, were of such a quality as to inspire instant devotion in the beholder. Those of the spectators, standing open-mouthed as the Holy Ghost descended, must have echoed my own as I regarded the picture. I grudged not a ducat that had been spent on materials, and would gladly have paid more. True to his word, however, Vernet refused the gift of money that I attempted to press upon him, and took only the sums that he had requested for materials.

As you all know, Vernet's depiction of the Baptism of Christ now forms one of the Duomo's greatest treasures, though Vernet's name is no longer attached to it, for reasons that will become apparent later.

Isaac has returned. His face appears to be an uncomfortable mixture of anguish and ecstasy, such as I have rarely seen. Isaac's eyes are wide, and his breathing is shallow and rapid. I have seen such things before, though, in those who have passed through extreme danger.

"Calm yourself, my friend," I tell him. "I see you are distressed. Sit, and tell me what has upset you."

Ali, the intelligent lad, has noted Isaac's state, and without being asked has brought refreshment.

"The blessings of Allah be upon you, Ali," says Isaac as he takes the beaker from the tray. As I have said, in this place all religions shimmer and merge like mirages in the desert sun.

"Some digitalis, Ali," I request. To Isaac, I say, "I have a little experience in medicine and curing men's ills. I believe that this will help restore some of your vitality."

Isaac's colour is returning, and his breathing becoming more regular. Even so, I shake a few drops of the foxglove juice that Ali has just brought me into Isaac's beaker, and request him to drink.

The drug takes almost immediate effect. His eyes lose their shining stare and take on a normal look, his breathing becomes more regular, and his whole body relaxes.

"Thank you," he says. "You are a true healer of bodies as well as of souls."

I smile. "I have some skill in that area," I confess.

"I will tell you what I have seen. The angel of which I spoke the other day..." He speaks in Latin.

"Yes, yes?" I do not even bother to conceal my impatience. "Ali, you may stay. I can tell you are eager to hear the story. Isaac, may I ask you to speak Arabic for Ali?" Ali thanks me, and squats beside my seat.

"He is no angel," says Isaac in his almost faultless Arabic. "He is possessed by a djinn. A demon. A creature of darkness. Or by a dybbuk."

I have not heard the last term before, and Isaac, in answer to my query, explains that the soul of a dead person can sometimes take over the body of a living man or woman.

"But why, my friend, why do you say this? Only the other day you were certain that you had seen a messenger of God. And now...?"

"He destroys. Destroys with fire." And so Isaac begins his tale. The stranger had appeared in the market, with no-one seemingly noticing whence or how he had appeared. For the space of some fifteen minutes, apparently, he had stood motionless, with none daring to speak to him or to approach him ("that is true," comments Ali, who is listening avidly to Isaac's recital, "my cousin Suleiman came by and told me the same just before you arrived"), as the news of his manifestation spread throughout the city.

Isaac had been informed of the angel's presence by a neighbour, and had hurried to the market, eager to see the angel who had excited him so strongly when he had first seen him.

After a time, the stranger moved, turning his head slowly towards a nearby butcher's stall. His hand moved, so Isaac relates, to his belt, from which he pulled what appeared to be a short dagger, which he held before him, pointing towards the stall on which he had fixed his gaze.

Without warning, fire leaped from the point of the weapon, Isaac tells us, shuddering as he tells us of these events. "And in the butcher's stall, one of the carcasses there burst into flame with a brilliant flash of light. We could all smell the burned flesh. 'Haram!' someone called. 'Unclean!' And so it was – it was the carcass of a pig. I knew the smell of a cooked pig from the time that I spent in Constantinople." Isaac, like me, has spent time in many places before coming to rest here.

"And what did the stall-keeper do?" I ask.

"By the time we had recovered our wits, the stall-keeper had vanished. If he had stayed, the crowd would have dragged him before the qadi. But what is more, the angel or demon or whatever he may be, had also vanished, even though he was surrounded on all sides by a great press of people."

"How had he achieved that?" Ali wonders aloud.

Isaac shakes his head. "Who knows? He was standing, as close to me as is that pomegranate tree there. We all looked at the burning pig – where else should we look? – and then he was no more. No-one remembers seeing him go. Only a demon could do such a thing."

I consider the matter. "It appears to me," I say at length, "that you may well have been correct when you first identified him as an angel. Firstly, there is the matter of his appearance and disappearance. It is clear that he possesses powers over and above those of ordinary men."

"So do djinns," objects Ali.

"Very true, Ali. I grant you that. But would a djinn seek to destroy that which was haram? Would he not rather encourage us to partake of it?"

Ali nods in approval of my words, but Isaac still remains unconvinced.

"But that dagger!" he says. "That is surely diabolical."

I shake my head and smile. "I must ask you to remember how, when Adam and Eve were expelled from Eden, how they were prevented from returning."

"A flaming sword," says Isaac slowly. "An angel with a flaming sword."

"Quite so. My dear friend, I believe you have given yourself a fright and endangered your health over a foolish trifle."

Isaac has the grace to smile weakly. "I am sorry for the trouble I have given you," he says. "And to you," to Ali.

"It is an honour to serve sages such as yourself and my master," says Ali, rising to his feet and bowing his head as he faces us. "Even if you are both infidels," he adds, with an impertinent grin, as he returns to the house.

Isaac and I both burst into loud laughter.

"I am pleased that we can share this together," I say to Isaac quietly. "Let us thank the Lord of Hosts for our lives."

Isaac leaves soon afterwards; an elderly Jew having been given spiritual comfort by an equally elderly Christian priest in the company of a Muslim.

I give thanks to Adonai, to the Holy Trinity, and to Allah, for the gift of friendship.

And I consider my fate. Was the burning of that unclean pig a warning to me, that my life could be taken as quickly and with as little compassion as was shown to that carcass? There is no defence. I must wait until the angel comes to me. There is nowhere to run. Nowhere to hide.

☾★

chapter 14 (Nessuna)

Vernet's "Baptism" was the talk of the city, and naturally Pietro was among those who came to admire it in its new home in the Duomo.

"A truly magnificent piece of work, is it not?" he said to me, stroking the head of the small furry monkey that clung to his shoulder, which I later discovered had been presented to him by a merchant who had sailed around the Western coast of Africa, in a search for a route to the fabled Spice Islands. "One can almost imagine oneself standing there."

"Yes, I was knocked sideways when I first saw it." My reply was deliberately colloquial, in contrast to Pietro's speech, which had often become more formal since he had attained a high position in the city's government. At first I had found it amusing, on a par with his affectations in dress and in habits (as, for example the aforementioned monkey), but lately it had begun to grate on my nerves a little.

Pietro frowned at my choice of words, but said nothing in direct response. "How much did he charge you for this sublime masterpiece?" he asked.

"Why, nothing," I said, enjoying his surprise at my reply.

Pietro's eyebrows shot up into his neatly-arranged, but already receding, hair. "A strange craftsman," he commented.

"However," I continued, "he was compensated for all the materials – the colours and so on – that he employed in the production of the painting. And they came to a tidy sum, I can tell you."

"I can well believe it," my friend answered, stepping forward to examine the picture more closely. "That is genuine lapis lazuli, is it not?"

"I sincerely hope so," I laughed. "The bills he presented to me would certainly seem to indicate that it is genuine. But I ask myself how he is to live, if he is not demanding payment for his work."

Pietro laughed. "I think I can answer your riddle," he told me. "This magnificent piece of work is the cheese in the mousetrap. Mice such as me," and he here made a mock-deprecatory moue, "will be attracted by the quality of the cheese, and will enter the trap, only to find that they must pay a price for future work. Not that I care, if he can produce a likeness of the Prefect that will truly reflect His Magnificence's nobility of character."

This was an outrageous piece of flattery on Pietro's part. The Prefect of whom he spoke was a venal old lecher, who had, by reputation, enjoyed the favours of many of the local maidens, and taken a large part of the city's wealth for himself. I held my tongue and smiled as innocently as I could manage.

"I am sure Vernet would be happy to entertain your request," I told him.

"Would you do me the favour of introducing me?" he asked. "It may be that the trap will close less forcefully on a mouse who is a friend of a friend."

"I would hardly consider myself a friend of Vernet's," I replied, taking Pietro's offered arm, avoiding the monkey (which had an unfortunate habit of pissing on those it considered unfriendly to its master), and we strolled out of the Duomo. To those who saw us, we presented a perfect picture of the spiritual and temporal powers of the city, united in friendship.

Vernet listened to Pietro's proposal with some enthusiasm. "A likeness of a living person as the main subject? And which saints and holy emblems do you consider would be appropriate for me to include with His Magnificence?"

"I feel this is more your department than mine, Gerardo," Pietro told me.

I thought rapidly. Demons of lust and cupidity seemed more

appropriate to my mind than did saints or holy symbols. I appeared to consider the matter for a while, and then spoke. "I feel His Magnificence should be surrounded by angels, bringing him the gifts of divine Wisdom and Prudence."

I am sure that Pietro recognised my true feelings, but he said nothing, other than to agree with me.

"Excellent," said Vernet. "That would be a simple task, other than for the fact that..." His voice tailed off, and he appeared to be somewhat at a loss.

"What is it?" both Pietro and I asked him.

"The women of your city are ... this is a most embarrassing matter for a guest to the city to repeat, but I fear I must speak the truth ... not of the comeliness I would expect of an angel. I must have a model for my work, you understand. It is not possible for me to summon angels in my head to be transferred to my pictures. I have seen no such angels during my time in the city."

"The angels must be female?" I asked.

"In this case, I believe so, yes. Young and beautiful female forms will form an attractive contrast with your Prefect who is, from what I have been able to perceive at a distance, not in the first flush of his youth."

I smiled. "I take your point, but if you are unable to find such models for your angels, should we not seek some other figures to accompany him in the picture?"

Pietro smiled. "I may be of assistance to you, Messere Vernet." Where, I wondered, had he learned that title? "Perhaps I might be able to introduce you to some who could serve as your models."

I had learned to hide my feelings when faced with surprising speeches or statements. It would be highly inappropriate, for example, if one's confessor were to burst into a fit of giggles at the recital of a supposed sin that he considered particularly amusing. Even so, my face must have shown my astonishment at Pietro's words.

"Never fear, Gerardo, I have sources of beauty, of which I am certain you are unaware. As, I believe, do some of your colleagues in the Church. Not you, of course, my friend," he added, still smiling. I was relieved that he did not class me with those priests who, while publicly subscribing to a vow of chastity, carried on most unchaste affairs with women of low reputation, and sometimes even with ladies of some quality. Though I was forced, thanks to my position, to listen to their confessions, and prescribe appropriate penances for them, it seemed to me that there was very little of true repentance in their confessions. Having heard rumours that the Bishop himself was also guilty of such transgressions, I was more than a little reluctant to bring these matters before him.

But this digression is scarcely relevant to the tale I am telling. Pietro and Vernet arranged a time and a place to meet in the next few days, following which Pietro would introduce these mysterious heavenly beauties. I was pointedly excluded from the invitation, and did not press the point.

The resulting likeness of the Prefect was, like the "Baptism", the talk of the city, and the multitudes that came to view it, not only from our city, but from those of many leagues' distance, thronged to the Great Hall in the Citadel, where the Prefect, well pleased with the gift of his likeness that Pietro had presented to him, had decided to exhibit it to the general public.

It stood, behind a rope barrier, with two armed guards in attendance during the hours when it was on show.

Now that the picture has vanished from the public gaze, probably forever, I feel I should include a description of it, and my impressions of this extraordinary work. For it was truly extraordinary. The Prefect himself was depicted in such a way that his venality was immediately apparent to those who sought to discover it, but hidden to those who wished to think well of him.

He was richly attired in his official robes, seated at a table, a quill in his hand, seemingly in the act of signing a decree or an ordinance. His sandbox, and the seal of the city, together with wax and an unlit candle, stood at his elbow. His eyes were fixed on one other unexplained object which also stood on the table, but I shall describe that later.

However, it was not the Prefect that the visitors flocked to see, but the two angels giving him the divine gifts of Wisdom and Mercy, clearly labelled as such in the chalices that were being proffered to this vain old man. There were two angels, but I suspected that they had been taken from the same model, since they shared identical features.

Their hair was of a shining brightness like the sun, and their faces shone like polished silver. Silver too were their garments, which were not the robes in which angels are usually depicted. Indecent as it may seem, these angels, though quite clearly female in their form, were clad in tight-fitting breeches, which revealed their lower limbs at the same time as concealing them. I am sure that it was this, as well as the clinging silver bodices in which the upper part of their bodies were covered, which had attracted the attention of the vulgar. The piercing blue eyes of the angels were directed towards the mysterious object on which the Prefect's gaze was likewise directed, but at the same time, the viewer of the picture had the strange impression that the angels were at the same time regarding him or her.

This curious device on the desk appeared to consist of two parts, with a cord connecting the two. It was clear, from the way in which Vernet had depicted it, that it was actually one, and not two objects. The first part resembled some sort of golden cap, studded with what appeared to be stones, each with thin cords attached. These cords led together to form a thicker cord, as tributary streams flow together to form a river, and this became the cord attaching this golden cap to the other part, which took the form of a silver box. This box was about two palms in length, and one in width, if the representation was accurate, and with what appeared to be coloured jewels set into one side.

However, as I have said, it was the representation of the angels which attracted most attention, and it proved to have been a wise decision to have posted the guards, since they were frequently employed in keeping the crowds from touching or rubbing the painting. It was a truly magnificent piece of craftsmanship, however, and I congratulated Vernet warmly on it when I next encountered him.

"Thank you, Your Reverence," he answered me, having by now learned the correct form of address. "But such praise is due to the Almighty who gives us our gifts, is it not?"

"Indeed so," I agreed. "And your angels? Where did you discover them?"

Vernet shook his head. "Alas, Your Reverence, I am unable to tell you. Not only am I bound by an oath not to disclose what I have seen, but I cannot tell you. Before Signor del Murano took me to meet the model – for as you have no doubt observed, I painted the same model twice – he bound a cloth about my eyes, before leading me to meet her. I cannot tell you where we were, even were I allowed to do so."

"And your oath forbids you from telling me what sort of woman she was? What language she spoke to you?"

"It does. Pray do not press me further on this subject, Your Reverence."

Naturally, I desisted. Far be it from me to force any man to break his oath. I was of the opinion, though, that Pietro, friend of mine though he professed to be, would likewise be unwilling to share this secret with me.

As a result of this image of the Prefect, several other prominent citizens professed their desire to have their likenesses taken by Vernet, but it transpired that only a few of them could afford the prices that he demanded for his work.

However, those who paid these prices were denied the company of angels. Even so, the likenesses that Vernet produced were true masterpieces, and were the pride and joy of those depicted in them.

Little did I know how Vernet's skills were being employed in a secretive and sinister manner.

✝

chapter 16 (Nessuna)

It is time to introduce another player in this story. Sister Maria was a nun of the Carmelite order, who had joined in her early life from a noble family in the adjoining city.

She was of sufficiently attractive an appearance that even her nun's habit could not hide it from the eyes of men. Even I, bound to celibacy, felt myself stirred by her beauty, which was not of the unearthly kind presented by Vernet's angels, but of a more earthly and immediate kind, infused with a spirituality that transcended the experience of most men. It was scarcely to be wondered that Pietro would be tempted, not just by her appearance and her beauty, but also by the fact that she was unattainable by reason of her vocation. It is a well-known fact that those fruits that hang just out of our reach are often the most desirable.

Not only Pietro, but the whole of the city was aware of her and her extraordinary appearance, and she attracted a crowd whenever she chose to attend Mass in the Duomo. This was a crowd of the vulgar that wished her no ill, or had any evil designs on her modesty, but simply wished to see the face of a saint, as she was popularly regarded.

It was therefore with a sense of great shock that Vernet's picture of which I speak was first exhibited. The subject was one from the Book of Daniel, "Susanna and the Elders", depicting the scene when Susanna is taking her bath, and is spied on by the elderly lechers. This was not a new subject to be depicted, though at the time it was not a common one, but Vernet's treatment of it verged on the obscene. In most representations, Susanna is a maidenly, if comely, figure, who protects her modesty. In this instance, though, Susanna displayed all her female charms with the wantonness of a common harlot. That in itself would be shocking enough, but the face was that of Sister Maria!

Some of the more credulous would have had us believe that the naked shapely figure attached to that lovely face was also that of Sister Maria, but I am able to state with some authority that that was not the case. I now feel able to do this from this remote time and place, without violating the secrecy of the confessional. Poor Sister Maria died of fever soon after the events I am describing here, and to the best of my knowledge she has no surviving relatives in the region of the city, even should my words travel the leagues to there.

As her confessor, I had come to know the young nun as an honest and truthful follower of the rules of her order. Though others in her convent sometimes told me of sins of impropriety, Sister Maria had never done so, though she had confessed to having fallen to other, trivial, temptations of a different nature from time to time. If she had removed her habit to pose as a model for Vernet, she would undoubtedly have regarded this as a sin, and she would have confessed it to me.

This was only one shocking aspect of the picture. The other was the appearance of the two Elders, who had been consumed by desire for the beautiful young woman, and spied upon Susanna as she bathed, before falsely accusing her of intimacy with a young man when she would not yield to their lusts. In this case, Vernet had given one of the Elders the face of the Prefect, and the other was a representation of another senior member of the Council.

Furthermore, in the background of the picture was an angel (who does not form part of the Biblical narrative) whose face and attire were those of the angels in the Baptism. Why? I asked myself, did Vernet continue to use the same image of this angel? which was like no other representation of God's messengers that I had encountered.

The implication was clear, and the sympathy of the crowd was with

Sister Maria, whom they believed had been the recipient of unwelcome attentions by these two. When the Prefect and Signor Giovanni went abroad, they were jeered, and even the guards around them could not prevent them from being pelted with filth on more than one occasion.

Pietro, when I questioned him, refused to provide details of the workings of the Council, and the attitudes prevailing there, citing reasons of state as the reason for his sealed lips.

I summoned Vernet to my rooms in the Bishop's Palace, in the hope that I could discover the truth of his motivation for creating such a scurrilous work, and with luck, to pour oil on the troubled waters that were apparently surging in the Council.

"Why," I asked him, "did you create such a picture? Surely you must have realised what a stir it would cause?"

A faint smile crossed his lips. "Indeed I did have my misgivings, Your Reverence, but I was assured that all would be well taken care of, and that any trouble would be swiftly wiped away."

"And who was it who gave you that assurance?"

"I cannot tell you."

"Cannot, or will not?"

"I swore a holy oath on the relics of St. Antony in the Duomo that I would not reveal who paid me to produce this picture, nor the terms of my engagement. Surely Your Reverence would not wish me to break such an oath."

I had my suspicions already as to who was responsible for this. "I may assume that you were well rewarded for your task."

"I was, Your Reverence."

"Then may I be permitted to offer you some advice? Pray, sit. Let me talk to you as man to man, not as a priest. I will not press you on the matter of your oath, but I have a very strong suspicion of who lies behind all this. But you are now in a very dangerous position, my friend." He started. "You know, no doubt, of the old saying that two may keep a secret if one of them be dead?"

"I do, Your Reverence."

"I believe the other party has no intention of departing this life."

"You are throwing me out of the city?"

"I am doing no such thing, and I have no authority to do so. I simply make an observation which you may heed or ignore as you please. You have talent, Vernet. That much is crystal clear to all who view your works. I would not wish to see such a talent cut down in the flower of its possessor's youth."

"You mean this? This is not some pretext dreamed up because you are offended by my representation of an incident in Holy Scripture, or by my rendition of certain personages?"

I shrugged. "I am offended, true, but the offence stems not simply from your work, as the use to which your work has been put, and the perversion in it, which I do not believe was your idea."

"It was not."

"Are you still under oath as to the identity of the model for your angel?"

"If I knew, which I do not, I would not be permitted to tell you."

"As I thought, then. Let me repeat my warning to you. Leave this city as soon as possible, and take your talent with you to delight others. Alternatively, remain here, with the probability of losing your talent, along with your life."

He bowed his head. "I thank Your Reverence for your consideration."

✝

chapter 17 (Lamakan)

I ask the Imam about the angel (or demon) in the market. He has not seen him, and therefore professes scepticism as to the events as related by Ali.

He agrees with my analysis of a fiery sword, however, making this a visitor from heaven rather than from hell, and the fact that an unclean pig was destroyed is further proof of the divine origin of the visitor.

I do not know what to believe. I am caught in a hell of doubt.

As for my future, I am still unsure as to whether I should run or I should stay here. I was sure of my decision when I told Vernet that he should leave the city. Now I am faced with a similar dilemma. Am I to leave the city, and wander through the desert, ever eastward, until I reach the end of the world, or am I to stay here and await my fate?

I am not as young as once I was – it's a truism that applies to us all – but the real truth of it only strikes home after one has reached a certain age, and that age is now in the past for me. I will stay and await whatever befalls me.

☪

Vernet too, stayed. He chose to ignore my warning, and continued to live in the city, but his life following our conversation was measured in days.

In the early morning of the third day after we had spoken, his body was discovered in the street, with some twenty or thirty dagger wounds. The stones of the street were red with blood, which despite all efforts to remove it, did not fully disappear until the autumn rains had come and gone.

I knew whom I suspected, and went to see him.

"Pietro," I asked him, after the usual polite preliminaries. "Why? The man had a God-given genius and talent. Why, in God's name."

"You have just answered your own question," he told me. "It was indeed in God's name. Do you think I was going to let such blasphemy to go unpunished?"

"Blasphemy is my province," I reminded him. "If I examined him and found he was guilty of heresy or blasphemy, it would be my responsibility to hand him over to the civil authorities for appropriate punishment."

Pietro laughed mirthlessly. "The Church does not spill blood, and therefore remains pure and holy. But there is another kind of blasphemy – against members of God's creation."

"Such as Sister Maria?" I asked. "I have not spoken to the poor girl about the matter, but I agree that the painting did not show her in the best possible light."

"On the contrary, it showed her in a very good light indeed." Pietro leered, with an expression such as those of the Elders depicted in the painting we were discussing.

"Now you are as bad as Vernet," I exclaimed, seriously annoyed by his flippant answer.

"Oh, I am worse, much worse, as I think you probably have realised by now. No, the true blasphemy of that piece lay in the depiction of the Prefect and Signor Giovanni. The mob's sympathies are all with the girl. The Prefect and Giovanni have been made out to be the worst kind of degenerates through that picture."

"And, between ourselves, is that not the case in reality?"

"It matters not whether it be true or false. What matters is the appearance as presented to the masses. And that picture presented an image of our leaders that is undesirable. Vernet's death is a convenient coincidence."

I inwardly questioned the use of the term "coincidence", but refrained from making any comment.

"Let us assume," I said, "that this picture actually does have the effect that you fear, and that the Prefect and Giovanni are forced to step down from their present positions. What then?"

"Why, the Council would have to appoint a new Prefect, of course."

"And who do you see as a likely candidate for that post?"

Pietro had the grace to appear slightly embarrassed, though embarrassment was probably the last emotion in his mind.

"I believe I would be regarded as the favourite, given the current composition of the Council."

"As I thought," I remarked. "Let us hope that it does not come to that pass for many years to come, though."

"Meaning?"

"Meaning, of course, that I trust the Prefect and Giovanni will continue in office, performing their tasks as admirably as they have been doing for the past years." I endeavoured to make my tone as light and innocent as possible. I very much doubt whether Pietro was fooled.

"A sentiment one might also apply to His Reverence, the Bishop." Pietro knew well that I had been as good as promised the bishopric upon the death of the incumbent. "His Reverence is in good health – for his age. I trust we will enjoy the benefit of his wisdom for several years to come," I agreed, as blandly as I could.

Pietro poured more wine for us both, and he and I sipped.

"I have another question for you, my friend," I said, breaking a silence of some minutes. "It concerns the angels in Vernet's pictures."

"What of them?"

"They are drawn from a living model?"

"They are. Further than that I am not at liberty to disclose."

There was a set to Pietro's jaw which made it clear that he was not prepared to go further into the matter. I started another angle of attack.

"What are we to do with Vernet's pictures?" I asked.

It seemed that Pietro had been expecting this question. "We must burn them all," he replied promptly.

"I agree with you regarding the most recent picture. The likeness of the Prefect also, if he agrees," I told him. "The portraits of the citizens and Councillors. But the Baptism must stay in the Duomo. I choose to believe that it was painted by a man of faith, and not by a diabolist."

"Very well," he said. "After this latest abomination, I think the Prefect will be happy to see an end to any traces of Vernet in his life, as will all the other citizens of whom Vernet created likenesses. As to the Baptism, I believe with you that it should remain, but with any association with Vernet removed from it. The people will soon forget."

And so it was that the magnificent painting of Our Lord's Baptism was saved, though when I last beheld it (and I weep silently to think that I will never see it again), it was ascribed to "An Unknown Painter".

"So," Pietro said after the last painting had been consigned to the flames. "All is now clear."

Part IV - Judges

chapter 19 (Nessuna)

The meaning of Pietro's words "All is now clear," revealed itself on my walk from his house to mine following that conversation. His meaning was undoubtedly that all was now clear for his eventual promotion to Prefect.

I mentioned before that Pietro was being considered for Sub-Prefect, or even (by a few) for Prefect, despite his relatively young age and lack of experience. However, another party held that Signor Giovanni would succeed to that lower position, given his seniority and the general regard in which he was held.

However, the next Council meeting produced some unexpected results.

I was present at this particular meeting, though it was not usual for me to do so. It was customary for the Bishop to attend, though he had no vote or voice in the workings of the Council, but on this occasion, he was suffering from a severe cold. I therefore attended in his stead.

Pietro greeted me warmly, a smile on his face. "I think we will see great things today," he said.

"I sincerely hope so, for your sake," I said. I was sincere, I think. As aware as I was of Pietro's many faults, as a governor of our city, or as his deputy, he was preferable to the current Prefect, and to many of the other Council members. He did, for example, possess intelligence and learning, which was not the case with many of the Councillors.

The Council took their assigned places on the benches lining the long Council board, and I sat on the bench at the back of the chamber, my pen and tablet ready to take notes.

At the appointed time, the bell of the Duomo struck the hour, and an expectant hush fell over the assembly, to be replaced after a short space of time by an excited buzz. The Prefect's chair was vacant.

"He was aware of this meeting?" someone asked.

"I informed him personally." It was Pietro who replied.

"Perhaps he has mistaken the time," another suggested. "Maybe one of us should visit his house and remind him of this meeting."

"Then you go, Luigi. I warn you, he can be like a bear with a sore head if he is awakened unexpectedly, especially if he has enjoyed a late night."

The Councillor left, but returned after only a few minutes – alone and in a state of great excitement.

"Is he coming to attend the Council?" was the question.

"No, and he will never attend another meeting," came the answer, "unless it is as a corpse at his wake. Gentlemen," and there was a catch in the speaker's voice, "His Magnificence has hanged himself."

There was uproar. I crossed myself, and I noticed many of the Councillors (but not Pietro) doing the same as I murmured a prayer for the soul of this man who had stolen God's gift of life.

Above the growing hubbub of voices, I could hear Pietro calling, "Is there any message for us?"

"There is. It was at his feet. Is it your wish that I read it to you?"

There was a chorus of "Aye", and the noise subsided as the Councillors resumed their places and listened.

"'I take my own life in the full knowledge that this is a sin against God and condemned as such by the Holy Church. However, I can no longer stand in front of the Council of this city, nor in front of its citizens, as a result of the humiliation that I have suffered in the recent past. I therefore bid you farewell, my friends and colleagues. May you serve the city better than did I.'"

Uproar broke out once more when this had been read out, and

many of the Councillors were openly weeping. Pietro (who else?) led a small party out, calling as they went that they would bring the body back to the Council chamber.

It was not long before they returned with their grisly burden. I rose from my place and closed the dead man's bulging bloodshot eyes. "Lux perpetua luceat ei, et dona ei pacem," I prayed. I realised that I was asking for absolution for one who had committed a grave sin, but I took his note to be a contrite confession, and my prayers for him to be a form of absolution. When I informed the Bishop later of my actions, he concurred, reminding me that charity towards sinners was more pleasing to God than their condemnation.

After a decent interval, the Council reconvened, with the Sub-Prefect, Filippo, taking the chair.

"The office of the Prefect now being vacant, do we elect Filippo to take his place?" Again, it was Pietro taking the lead here. I admired his nerve, given that I knew he was angling for the larger prize of the Prefecture himself. He must have felt that Filippo's nomination would be rejected by the Councillors.

There was what seemed like a unanimous concert of "Aye", and my heart inwardly sank, though I joined in the congratulations and ap-plause that greeted the appointment. Filippo was no fool, and far from sharing the love of vice that had characterised his predecessor.

On the contrary, he was known as being guided by a strictly moral compass. So strict indeed that when he appeared on the streets of the city, the majority of citizens would take another path to avoid meeting him, for fear of a reproof regarding their manner of dress or behaviour. He had, on one notorious occasion, even reprimanded the Bishop for the amount and quality of the fur trimming his robe.

All in all, I could foresee trouble ahead with this man as the ruler of the city. Our citizens were (and presumably still are) creatures of the moment. For the most part God-fearing, but delighting in the enjoy-ment of His gifts, rather than in blind obedience to His laws.

As for Pietro, I knew him well enough to realise that whatever ex-pression he chose to adorn his face, the set of his jaw, and the stiff set of his shoulders showed his fury. Surely, I thought, even Pietro was not arrogant enough to believe that he would be selected as Prefect following such an event as had just occurred.

After thanking the assembly for their confidence in him (and whatever else one might say of him, he was no long-winded speaker, but gave his opinions in brief, almost terse, sentences), Filippo addressed the company "My first act as Prefect is to declare my deputy. I therefore commend Signor Giovanni to you gentlemen. All those in favour?"

There was a chorus of "Aye" from approximately all of those present. I noticed that the gathering had almost imperceptibly split into two groups; one around Giovanni, and one, smaller, around Pietro.

"Those against?"

The chorus of "Nay" was noticeably less strident and was quieter than that which had acclaimed Giovanni.

"I therefore declare that Signor Giovanni is the new Sub-Prefect of the city."

Giovanni rose to his feet, and I, for one, sighed inwardly, as I prepared myself for a blast of florid oratory.

"Most esteemed colleagues, and may I say friends of many years, I am deeply sensible of the great honour you have done me by bestowing your trust and confidence on me in such a manner, and that you have seen fit to award to me the second-highest honour that the city can bestow on one of its citizens. However..." (and you could almost hear a pin drop as Giovanni's voice, usually confident in its turn of phrase, faltered and became almost inaudible) "...however, I am unable to take the position." He stopped, and the silence became absolute.

A shout from the benches. "Shame on you, Giovanni. Why?"

"Shame on me, indeed," he replied. "The same shame that led our brother," and he gestured towards the shrouded corpse that lay on a board at the back of the chamber, close to where I was sitting, "to take his own life. I therefore, with the greatest gratitude, and not a little reluctance, nonetheless feel that I do not deserve that confidence and trust. Thank you."

He sat down, and once again, the chamber was filled with the up-roar of confused Councillors. I caught sight of Pietro's face, and for a fleeting moment glimpsed the sneer of triumph that filled it, before he replaced the expression with one of concern and sympathy as he talked to his group of friends.

Surely this would lead him to the place of Sub-Prefect? And shortly after that, if Prefect Filippo lived up to his reputation of enforcing strait-laced morality, he would be requested to step down very soon. Which left Pietro as the obvious replacement – at an age where he was not even permitted to be a member of the Council.

He stood forward, confident in the expectation that his name would be put forward as the next Sub-Prefect. His confidence was rewarded, and one of his supporters called out the recommendation.

As Prefect, Filippo put the motion to a vote, but it seemed that the "Nays" outnumbered the "Ayes", and the look of fury on Pietro's face, which he took no pains to conceal, was almost terrifying.

"Whom do you nominate, then?" asked Filippo.

"Why, Daniele."

This time, the vote went Daniele's way, and Pietro was forced to leave with a bad grace. "See me at my house later tonight," he hissed at me as he fairly slunk out of the chamber, leaving behind him a mass of gossiping Councillors.

Naturally, I made my way that evening to Pietro, where I discovered him slumped at a table, a half-empty wine flask in front of him, and two other flasks, now emptied of their contents, to one side.

Without rising, he lifted his head, and greeted me, bleary-eyed.

"Ah, my friend Gerardo," he slurred. "My oldest and my truest friend. Come, drink." He stretched out a hand to the flask and made as if to pour the contents into a goblet, but his hand was shaking so badly that I felt compelled to take the wine from him and pour it myself.

"What happened?" he asked me. "You were there. You saw it. Why did they not select me?" He raised his goblet to me, and I returned the gesture.

"Because you are not of age?" I suggested.

He looked at me closely, blinking. "Do you believe that?"

I shrugged. "No matter what they truly feel, this is the only answer you are likely to receive from those who did not support you."

"So you feel there may be other reasons?"

"A plethora of them. Jealousy will be the chief, I feel. A young man, more intelligent and more attractive in so many ways than are they," this produced a wan smile, "who is obviously ambitious, is bound to produce some resentment. Surely you can see that for yourself?"

"I grant you that. But to select that doddering old fool Daniele as the Sub-Prefect! You know what will happen in the next few months, do you not?"

"No-one knows what will happen in the future, save for God, and He has not informed me."

"Then let me take His place." I forgave Pietro his minor blasphemy as he continued. "Filippo is, let us be blunt here, a pain in the arse. His view of morality may coincide with that of the Church. Of course I know," he held up a hand to stop the protest that I had already refrained from making, "that in practice you and the other clergy are not as literal or as fanatical in their promotion of these things as is he. But now that he has control of the Council, and will impose his beliefs on the whole city as a result, I foresee that he will become deeply unpopular in a matter of mere months. And then..." He drew the edge of his hand across his throat.

"And you would then have become Prefect, of course."

"Of course."

The conversation lapsed into silence for some time, during which my goblet was drained and refilled once, and Pietro's twice.

"Did you expect the late Prefect, God rest his soul, to take his own life?" I asked suddenly.

Pietro answered the question before he had had time to consider. "No. I expected him to resign his post. It was as much of a shock to me as it was to anyone when the news came to us."

"And Giovanni?"

"It was a gamble. I expected him to decline the position of Prefect, but I could not be sure."

Though I was certain that Pietro was behind these machinations, I did not expect him to make a full confession to me, nor did he do so.

"At any rate," I told him, "you are further up the ladder than you were." I have found that expressing sympathy, rather than condemnation, with sinners' motivations often leads to an opening of their hearts.

Pietro shrugged. "I suppose that is true. But how long must I wait? How many years?" The naked ambition in this cry of desperation shone through, and it frightened me.

We relapsed into silence again, and drank, studiously avoiding each other's gaze. As I cast my eye about the room, it lit on a strangely familiar object.

"What is that?" I asked Pietro, pointing to the cap and reliquary that had appeared in the picture of the late Prefect, which now stood in a recess in a darkened corner of the room.

Pietro's face turned as hard as stone. "Gerardo, my old friend," he answered me, and there was nothing of friendliness in his voice, "pray do not ask any further questions about this. It is a matter that does not concern you."

The tone in which he spoke these words admitted of no argument, and I therefore forbore from questioning him further on the matter, but it seemed strange to me that the strange object that had been depicted with the late Prefect (for I was sure that it was the same) should now find itself with Pietro.

My question seemed to have put an end to any further conversation, and I left Pietro's house shortly after finishing my wine.

chapter 21 (Lamakan)

ƒatima has just announced that the angel/demon called while I was at prayer yesterday. He asked for me by the name by which I had been known in the past. Fatima, of course, does not know that former identity of mine, and therefore informed the stranger that no-one by that name resides here.

Upon hearing this, apparently the stranger then proceeded to give a brief, if somewhat flattering, description of me as a younger man (which I will not trouble you with here), which Fatima grudgingly admitted might be a description of my former self.

"But I said to him, master, that I was not sure, and that he was probably mistaken," she informs me. Poor girl, he has no idea of what she may have done. Perhaps I should tell her and Ali to search for a new master.

"And what did he say?"

Fatima gives me the bad news. "He will come again tomorrow after zuhr, the noon prayer. He told me that he would wait for you if you were not in."

So. It is given to me, as it is not given to many, to know the date and time of my death. For I have no doubt that this demon from the North is here for one thing only — to dispose of me and silence me for ever.

☪

chapter 22 (Nessuna)

Our life in the city proceeded. Our Bishop died, and I, as expected, was chosen by the Archbishop to fill his place.

Pietro was one of the first to congratulate me, though, being Pietro, there was more than a little self-interest in his words.

"Now you are elevated to the giddy heights, I hope you will be able to use your influence to advance me," he said.

I told him that I was not sure that my influence was as great or as far-reaching as he seemed to believe, but reassured him that if any opportunity presented itself to promote Pietro, I would use it.

For Pietro's prediction had failed to come true. The self-righteous Prefect Filippo had failed to make himself sufficiently unpopular, and still retained his position, as did Sub-Prefect Daniele, leaving Pietro frustrated and fuming. Sufficient time had now passed that he was legally permitted to be a Councillor, and therefore assume these higher offices, but the holders obstinately refused to give up their positions to allow him to take their place.

As for the position of the Bishop (that is to say, myself), I found that I was more in conflict with Filippo than I had expected. I had already marked him as a self-righteous long-winded bore, but he insisted on our holding weekly meetings, which could have dealt with the business of the city in thirty minutes, but invariably took up half the day or more. On occasion, I was forced to invent a wedding or a funeral for which I had to prepare in order to avoid having the whole day wasted.

Take, for example, the case of the pointed shoes. A fashion had just come in, from Rome or Naples or I know not where, for men to wear shoes with pointed toes, the longer the better. They looked absurd, but the young men of the city who could afford such things were in raptures over them, with some taking the fashion to such extremes that the toes of the shoes were attached by little chains to garters worn just above the knee.

"It is the sin of vanity, Bishop," thundered the Prefect for the tenth time that morning. "You must preach a sermon against this slavish following of an obscene and ridiculous fashion, thereby showing the wearer to be in league with the Devil." Quite apart from the absurdity of such a claim, the fact that he was bellowing at me like a cowherd to his charges made me less likely to be sympathetic to his views. I said nothing, but regarded my visitor, clad in a silk doublet, trimmed with golden lace. As with so many of his kind, he was impervious to any irony, and started to continue his rant, but I held up my hand.

"Your Magnificence is concerned with this matter, but for myself, I do not see that it is of any great consequence, other than that it is inconvenient, and possibly dangerous to the wearer should he chance to trip and fall."

"But the vanity, Bishop! The sin!"

I sighed. "Sin brings its own rewards. There are more serious matters that you might be bringing to my attention, such as the exorbitant interest rates that I hear are being charged to some of the smaller shopkeepers in the city."

"The Jews are at it again, then?" sneered the Prefect. "We should enact an ordinance to expel them from the city. I trust such a move, at least, would have your backing?"

"In this case, your Magnificence, the usury is being carried out by those who profess themselves to be Christians, some of whom are members of the Council. The Jews are innocent of this crime, which I consider to be of significantly more importance than the length of our citizens' shoes. Such a move would not have my backing, and I would refer you to certain words in Holy Writ with regard to the hospitality due to strangers, as well as Our Lord's attitude towards the money-changers in the Temple."

He flinched a little at the rebuke, but said nothing, and, to my dismay, returned to the topic of dress, but this time the use of fur trimming on women's robes. This topic, too, soon burned itself out, and it appeared that the Prefect had mercifully run out of topics, when he suddenly changed the subject completely.

"Tell me in confidence, Bishop. You are friends with Pietro – Pietro del Murano, as he has recently taken to styling himself – are you not?"

"I am, and have been since childhood."

"He is ambitious, and covets my position, I know. But he will not have it," and there was a touch of anger in the old man's voice as he said these words, "until I am ready to let it go, and Daniele has likewise surrendered his position. If you can tell him that, I would be grateful. It might make him a better Council member, concentrating on city business, rather than on his own ambition."

I smiled. "I think I can manage to convey that message to him." I sat back and waited. When you have heard as many confessions as have I, you develop a sense of when there is something more that the other wants to tell. There is no point in trying to coax it out of them – all you can do is wait until they are ready. And so it was with the Prefect.

"Do you believe," he said, in a rush of embarrassment, "that your friend might be a traitor to the city?"

I picked my words carefully. "I believe that he could be, if he sincerely believed that he was acting for the betterment of the city." I did not expound further on this, because I was convinced that Pietro's concept of a better state of affairs for the city involved Pietro's being at its head. "However," I went on, "I do not believe that he is currently engaged in any such activity."

"You would tell me if you did so believe, or if you had knowledge, would you not, Bishop?"

"Naturally." There was more to come, and I waited expectantly. Sure enough, the Prefect stirred in his seat, and after a little hesitation, continued.

"What if I told you that I had knowledge that he was in collusion with forces outside the city?"

I was puzzled. "Why, what sort of forces exist outside our city?"

"I am not sure, but I have witnesses. One of my men brought a report before me which stated that he observed Pietro del Murano meeting a northerner in a little wood outside the city." I had previously been aware that Filippo employed several agents to act as his eyes and ears, but I was more than a little surprised to learn that he was using them to keep watch over his fellow Councillors.

"A northerner?"

"I believe he was talking to one of those Norse barbarians who came from Thule and invaded Sicily so many years ago and now have so much influence in the south of Italy."

I was curious. "What leads you to that belief?"

"According to my informant, the man to whom Pietro was talking was clad in silver armour. He was at least a head taller than Pietro, who, as you well know, is of above average stature himself."

"And his face? Was he bearded, as these northerners so often are?"

"My informant could not see his face. However, he reported that his hair was golden, and worn long, in the fashion of these Norsemen."

"And since he could not see his face, I assume that he could not hear their conversation."

"Sadly, no. But what else could they have been discussing other than treason? What other reason would a Councillor of this city have to talk with one from outside, alone, outside the city walls?"

"Where exactly did this take place?"

The Prefect described the place where I had remarked the strange circles and indentations following Pietro's visit there some years previously. "Maybe he was engaged in some sort of trade?" I suggested.

"It is possible," he admitted. "My man reported that some object was passed between them."

"In which direction?"

"A good point, Bishop. From what he could observe, it was from the barbarian to Pietro. Payment, no doubt, for our Councillor's treachery."

"You seem to be convinced of his guilt, Your Magnificence."

"I am fairly persuaded, yes."

"Then why do you not summon him to answer these charges in open Council?"

There was a silence, which I knew was the precursor to another admission. "Because I am not sure, and should I be proved wrong, it would damage my reputation still further. You know, do you not, of my lack of success in banning the annual Carnival? Although I am Prefect, the Council advised me that any move to stop the Carnival would not be sympathetically received by the citizens. My prestige within the Council has suffered as a result. If I were to make an accusation against a fellow Councillor which could not be proved, that would further diminish my standing."

Pride. Always damnable pride. I am subject to it myself at times, I admit, but so often it seems that those who make the greatest show of their righteousness are those who are affected most by it.

After the meeting, I reflected on what the Prefect had told me. He had not forbidden me to mention the matter to Pietro, and I thought it prudent to advise my friend of His Magnificence's suspicions.

To my surprise, he laughed when I told him of my conversation with the Prefect.

"Thank you, Gerardo," he smiled. "But I was already aware of that suspicion. Just as the Prefect has his eyes and ears, so I have mine. If he decides to bring his suspicions before the Council, rest assured that I have the means to ensure that such a hearing will never take place."

"And the meeting with a stranger?"

"The Prefect's man never saw the face of my correspondent, did he?"

I wordlessly agreed with a nod of my head.

"I met with no Norseman, and I will take my oath on the Bible regarding that fact, should you desire it," he stated simply.

"But someone from outside the city?"

"Certainly. But no enemy of our city. Again, I will swear an oath on that."

"And what, if anything, was passed between you? Money?"

"Not at all. Something of little financial value, but of great utility. It is not anything that will cause harm to our city, or the Church. Allow me a few secrets, if you please, Gerardo." He smiled, and there was some genuine warmth in his expression.

So I left the matter, but I felt that Filippo, pompous old windbag that he was, had brought up matters which merited my attention.

chapter 23 (Nessuna)

It was therefore with some interest that I received a visit from Fabio of the Prefectural Guard (the same Fabio who carried out the arrest with which I began my narrative) just after sundown, some months after the conversation I described just now.

I had not yet retired, being engaged in some correspondence with the Holy See regarding some of the priests whom Rome wished to transfer into my diocese, and whom I had no wish to admit.

"Your Reverence's pardon for disturbing you at this hour," Fabio said, "but I thought you should know that Bernardo saw Signor Pietro making his way to the hollow outside the city walls. You asked for one of us to inform you should such a thing occur in the future."

"I did, but that was some years ago, and I had completely forgotten that I had made such a request. Even so," I said, and hurriedly donned a large dark cloak. "You will accompany me, Fabio?"

"I fear that my duties prevent me. Do you feel you will be in any danger? If so, I can ask one of my men to accompany you."

"I thank you for the thought, but I feel I will be safe."

"Don't say I didn't warn you, Your Reverence." Fabio said. He had been in my service before joining the Prefectural Guard, and I thereby permitted him these occasional moments of familiarity.

I bundled my cloak about myself, casting the hood over my head, and slipped out of the house through the streets to the gate of the city.

One of the guards, who had obviously been warned of my possible arrival by Fabio, wordlessly nodded and allowed me to slip through the gate. "Don't worry, Your Reverence. We'll let you back in again when you return," he chuckled as I passed him a coin.

I approached the clearing cautiously, but before I reached it, I could hear Pietro's voice, singing. He had retained, as I mentioned earlier, a particular purity of tone, and his treatment and interpretation of even the simplest song could move even the most stony hearts. Why, I asked myself, would he wish to sing here, alone? Or was he alone? I could not see, and cautiously moved closer, cursing silently every time my clumsy feet trod on a twig that cracked under my weight.

I saw the other before I saw Pietro. As the Prefect had told me, Pietro was consorting with a tall, fair-haired stranger. What Filippo did not know, and what I now knew, was that the stranger was female. Not only was she female, she was quite clearly the model for the angels depicted by the late painter, Vernet. She was standing, her face turned towards me, but cast slightly down.

Like the depiction of the angels, she was clad in a close-fitting silver garment, which left one in no doubt as to her sex. Her face... How do I describe her face? Vernet had come some way in his representation of the beauty of her countenance, but it was nothing when compared to the actuality. One sometimes encounters a beauty that can terrify, such as on this occasion, and I began to understand the fear and confusion of the prophets when they were visited by angels. Her eyes were piercing, as Vernet had delineated them, but far more awesome than he had dared to make them (or was capable of representing them), for truly, there was about her that which was clearly inhuman. However, I was far from being convinced that this was a heavenly visitor. There was something about her and her attitude which did not speak to me of Heaven.

I moved slightly closer and beheld my friend, facing away from me, his head thrown back, singing a song of courtly love which had been all the rage the previous year, when it had been introduced to the city by a wandering troubadour. He was, as the Prefect had informed me, somewhat smaller than his companion, and it was for that reason that she was facing slightly downward, those wondrous eyes of hers fixed on his face.

I confess to being so entranced by the magic of Pietro's singing that I forgot all time, lost as I was in the beauty of the music. At length, it stopped, and the spell was broken. There was a hush, broken only by the sound of a distant crow calling to its fellows.

The stranger spoke, in our language, but strangely accented, with a lilt to it that I had never heard before.

"Thank you," she said, and the sound of her voice was as a silver trumpet, and the smile she bestowed on my friend was that of liquid fire. "My friend, you have well earned your reward tonight." So saying, she held out her hand with something – I know not what – in it, which Pietro accepted, and slipped into his sleeve.

"The pleasure is mine, Muriel," he said, with a low bow. "When will I have the pleasure of meeting you again?"

"I will let you know by the usual means," she answered in that thrilling and yet terrible voice.

I determined that it was time for me to leave, and I therefore made my way back to the city, taking a different route, guessing that Pietro would be taking the route by which I had arrived, that being the fastest and most convenient.

As I made my way to the gates of the city, I saw Pietro in front of me, but to my surprise, he avoided the main gates of the city, and made for the small postern, which was usually kept locked. Though I was some distance from him, and dusk was falling, I was able to discern that he withdrew a key from his cloak to unlock the small gate, though which he slipped furtively.

I returned through the gate by which I had left the city, and Fabio expressed his relief at seeing my return. "Did you find out anything interesting, Your Reverence?" he asked.

I was not about to gratify his curiosity. "Nothing of importance," I told him, pressing a coin into his hand with the advice that it be used to buy drink for all the guards who had been on duty with him that evening.

chapter 24 (Nessuna)

It was two days after that when the Prefect issued his new proclamation. I first heard about it from one of my chaplains, who came to me in a state of great excitement.

"Your Reverence, it's the Prefect!" he gasped. The poor fellow had obviously run too fast and too far for his health, and was wheezing and gasping.

"Sit down, breathe slowly, and calm yourself," I told him. "The Prefect, you say? Is he coming to visit?"

Breathless, Father Alberto shook his head.

"He is visiting?"

Another shake of the head.

"Then what?" I asked.

"He ... has ... gone ... mad!" exclaimed the priest, still breathing heavily.

"Come, tell me more," I said, pressing a glass of water into his hand.

"He has passed an ordinance forbidding the wearing of the colours red or blue or yellow, other than by members of the Council. Purple is to be reserved for His Magnificence alone."

"That places me in a slightly awkward position, since my office demands the wearing of purple."

"The same thought had also struck me, Your Reverence."

"And what are the penalties for those who disobey this order?" I asked.

Father Alberto shuddered. "At the worst, death or exile. The offender will be given the choice."

"Apparently Filippo believes that living outside this city is equivalent to death," I smiled.

"But for lesser offences, a heavy fine, and a whipping through the streets."

I thought for a moment. "How did you hear of this?"

"Signor Pietro del Murano told me about it first, but then I read the proclamation nailed up in the marketplace. At first, I thought that the Councillor was joking when he told me – you know his sense of humour…"

"All too well," I answered.

"…but it seems that this is a genuine proclamation."

"And the reaction of the people?"

"Anger. I overheard some of the conversations. Many of the crowd were all in favour of going with torches to His Magnificence's house, and setting fire to it, with him inside."

"That must never happen," I said, rising to my feet. "We have work to do. Fetch two acolytes to carry candles, and you, Father, to carry the crucifix before me when we go to the marketplace. And my valet, if you please."

I was dressed in my cope and mitre, and carried my crozier as our little procession made its way to the square, where a crowd was assembling. As Alberto had said, there was an ugly mood, and there were voices raised in anger, which stilled somewhat as we approached.

"What do you think of all this business, Your Reverence?" asked one of the crowd, pointing at a piece of paper stuck on the wall.

"I am on my way to see His Magnificence in an attempt to persuade him to rescind this order," I announced, to great cheers. "But," I held up a warning hand, the the noise ceased, as the waters of the Red Sea obeyed Moses when he stretched out his hand, "I had heard that some of you were threatening violence against the Prefect."

There were angry mutters. "Who does he think he is, telling us what colours we're allowed to wear?" one man shouted out angrily, and there was a chorus of assent. "Bastards like that, who don't know how the ordinary people live, shouldn't be allowed to tell us how to run our lives." The murmur of assent now grew in volume, till it sounded like a pack of angry beasts about to fall on their prey.

"You must not take life or harm others," I protested.

"And who do you think you are to tell us? Just because you're a bishop," came the same voice which had been shouting out against the Prefect.

"He's all right," came another voice. "His father was Giovanni, the shoemaker. He's one of us underneath all that fancy clobber. If anyone can make the Prefect see sense, it's His Reverence." The noise of the angry beasts lessened.

"Thank you, my friends. Give me a chance to see what I can do." The crowd parted (Moses again!) and let me through to the Prefect's house.

He received me coldly, in his study.

"I can guess why you're here," were his first words to me. "I suppose you can keep all your purple regalia and so on – I don't want an argument with the Church."

"You seem to be intent on picking a fight with the people, though," I pointed out.

"It is sinful for them to be wearing colours which are clearly reserved for their betters," he retorted.

I sighed. When men get this way, there is no reasoning with them. "I think you would be better off forgetting the whole business."

His coolness turned to anger. "Who are you to advise me?"

"One who is concerned for your welfare. The mob will burn down your house with you inside it should you continue along this path."

"Peasants!" he spat. "The Guards will protect me."

"They might try to protect you," I conceded. "But I would lay odds that they might not be quite so diligent in their efforts as you might hope. And even if they did resist whole-heartedly, they might not succeed."

"So my life is in danger, you say? What does Your Reverence advise? That I should withdraw my proclamation? That I should resign my position? Perhaps I should leave the city? Or even take my own life, as did my predecessor?" His sarcasm came to the fore as he spat out these sentences.

I spread my hands in what I hoped would be seen as a gesture of helplessness. "That is for Your Magnificence to decide. I would hardly recommend the last course of action, however."

Filippo laughed bitterly. "I am made of different stuff. My will is implacable. I shall not change my mind. Quod scripsi, scripsi, Bishop."

"Then allow me to administer the Last Rites to you, in the event that I never see you alive again."

He glared furiously. "You dare to threaten me?"

"I do no such thing," I answered as mildly as I could. "I merely make an observation."

"Ha!" He flung himself back in his chair, obviously deep in thought. Outside the house, the noise of the mob could be heard, increasing in volume. With a start, the Prefect rose to his feet. "I have decided. I shall never rescind my proclamation. That is for my successor to do. I hereby resign my office. Here." He removed the ceremonial chain of office and handed to me. "And here." He took the Great Seal of the city from the table and handed it me. "Daniele shall become the new Prefect and he can do what he likes with the proclamation. As for my future, since you seem to be the crowd's favourite, I look to you to ensure my safe passage out of the city in two hours' time. If you do not, my blood will be on your hands."

"I give you my word that you will be allowed to leave in safety."

He nodded. "Now go. Tell the rabble that they have won. The forces of sin have overwhelmed those of God, and you may be ashamed of yourself, Bishop, for allowing this to happen in our city. Now go. Go!"

He screamed the last words at me in an almost insane fury, and I scrambled out of that house, still grasping the chain and Seal that marked the office of Prefect. As I emerged from the doorway, the crowd saw me, and an expectant hush fell over the square.

"Friends," I called, holding up my hands to display the emblems of office. "My friends, Signor Filippo is no longer Prefect of this city."

There were cheers. "He will be leaving the city in two hours' time." More cheers. "And you are to allow him to depart in safety with no violence on your part. I have given my word that this will be so. Do you give me your word?"

It took a little time, but I received the assurances I demanded.

The exit of Filippo from the city was one of the saddest spectacles I have ever witnessed. He came down the steps of his house, dressed in the purple he had attempted to reserve for himself, and the crowd parted to make a narrow passage for him. As he walked through the crowd, he was obviously attempting to bid the citizens farewell, but they turned their backs on him as he approached, and refused all dealings with him. I, who was following some paces behind, witnessed all this, and also saw those who had turned their backs on the Prefect turn back to face me, with words and gestures of thanks for my intervention.

As we approached the walls, Fabio, who was in charge of the guard, silently ordered the gates to be opened, and Filippo stepped through them for the last time. He turned to face me.

"You kept your word, then, Bishop. Congratulations on your mastery of these scum." He spoke softly, so that only I could hear his words. "Pray for me," he added unexpectedly. "I do not know what comes next." So saying, he set off down the road to the next city. I watched until he was nearly out of sight, and then turned back. The crowd had dispersed, and, as I discovered later, were busily engaged in looting and ransacking Filippo's house.

✠

chapter 25 (Lamakan)

Waiting is hard at any time. Waiting for one's own death is not easy. I must tell the rest of my story, compressed as it may be, before my nemesis arrives and silences me for ever.

I have told Fatima and Ali that they may need to search for a new master soon. With tears in his eyes, Ali asked me if I intended to leave him soon. Of course, that is not true – I have no intention of leaving – it is something that has been forced on me, but such equivocation is probably beyond the lad's comprehension. I have sent him to invite the Imam to visit me, and he returns now with my guest.

"Salaam," I greet him in the fashion of this place.

"Salaam aleikum," he replies.

Ali brings mint tea, and we sit sipping our drinks, comfortably enjoying the silence that exists between friends.

"I may be leaving soon," I tell him.

He says nothing, but raises his eyebrows.

"In fact, it is almost certain that I will be leaving," I tell him.

"Will you be going far?"

"As far as it is possible for a man to travel," I answer. "The longest journey that a man can take."

He ponders this for a moment. "You are being forced to take this journey? It is not one that you are undertaking of your own will?"

I shake my head. "It is wished upon me."

"And there is nothing I can do to keep you here? I have friends in the guards of the Caliph (may he live forever). Something could be arranged."

"I fear they would not be able to prevent my leaving. Hence I called you here to bid you farewell."

"I am deeply sorry to hear that, my friend. I have learned much from you, and your presence and conversation have given me great pleasure."

"I may say the same of you." Seized by a sudden impulse, I take his hands in mine, and look into his eyes. "Tell me, are you frightened of this ultimate journey that we must all make?"

He smiles softly, and makes no attempt to remove his hands from mine. "The start of the journey may be painful," he answers. "The journey itself? Who knows? But the destination? Both you and I have descriptions of it, and though they differ, both are delightful. So, to answer your question. Yes, I am a little frightened of the journey, but I eagerly anticipate my safe arrival at the end of it."

I release his hands and sit back. "Thank you. You have given me strength."

There is little more to be said. Strange, that I, a bishop, should receive spiritual consolation from one I was brought up to believe as a heathen and a pagan. I am happy that I have learned this before I die.

☪

Part V - Kings

With Filippo gone, Daniele was immediately proclaimed Prefect, and his first act, on my advice, was to take a vote in the Council to rescind Filippo's absurd order on the colours of the garments that our citizens were allowed to wear.

The order to rescind was passed unanimously, with no debate. Following this, and flushed with success, Daniele proceeded to repeal several of Filippo's more unpopular edicts.

The next order of business for the Council was to elect a new Sub-Prefect. Pietro was the only candidate, and though I heard there were some mutterings against his appointment (I could not be present at the meeting of the Council, but sent one of my chaplains to represent me, as I had represented my predecessor), he was elected by a sizeable majority of those present.

Effectively, this gave Pietro supreme power in the city. Daniele, though he had been a Council member for many years, appeared ignorant of many of the formalities and procedures associated with the office of Prefect. These things were meat and drink to Pietro, and he managed to guide Daniele through the thorn bushes of Council meetings, with the outcome invariably being one for which Pietro had previously expressed approval, either openly, or privately to me. Somewhat to my discomfiture, I found that Pietro was increasingly being given credit for Filippo's departure from the city.

At the same time, Pietro's personal life became notorious. One evening, I confronted him with the gossip and rumours that surrounded him.

"No-one objects to a little wine," I told him, "but if the gossips are correct, you have been drinking more than a little. I was told that you were discovered the other night with your head in the fountain, and might even have drowned if you hadn't been pulled out."

"Guilty as charged," Pietro said. "But," he added, laying his hand on my arm, and breathing wine fumes over me, "allow me to say a few words in mitigation. Daniele is one of the most excruciatingly boring men I have ever had the misfortune to meet."

"He is a good man," I said.

"Oh, good, good, good. What is good? I tell you that the man has a mind as deep as a puddle of rain after a spring shower. He can string a few pretty words together when needed, true, as long as someone provides him with the thoughts to be clothed in those words, and that is hard work, I can vouch for it."

I nodded. "I had guessed that it was your mind behind these things. The recent law that now forbids men to beat their wives if they are discovered in adultery?"

"Yes, that is mine. I do not see that the Church can object to that, given Jesus' reaction to the woman taken in adultery. 'Let him who is without sin,' and so on."

"Very well," I said. "I have never approved of wife-beating under any circumstances, in any case. What about the removal of the penalty for sodomites?"

"There is still a penalty," he pointed out. "No longer death, but a fine."

"Derisory," I objected. "And if I may turn this conversation in the direction of the personal, I would like to ask if this has anything to do with other rumours that come my way, regarding your companions of the night."

"My dear Gerardo, that is a matter between me and my confessor, and quite frankly, none of your business."

"And the stories about you and the daughter of Tomaso, the stone-mason, who once was expecting your child, and now is not?"

He set his cup down on the table with such force that the wine spilled from it. "Who is telling those tales to you?"

I shrugged. "It is common gossip, I believe."

"Have you nothing better to do with your time than listen to common gossip? Do you spend your time in the marketplace, listening to the old women spreading their lies?"

"You know very well that I do no such thing."

"In which case, I demand to know who told you."

"I cannot remember."

"Tell me. I demand it!"

"Why? If it is a lie, then it is as nothing, smoke in the wind. If true—" I broke off. There was a look in Pietro's eye which spelled danger to one who had crossed a line that he had drawn. "Very well, if I remember rightly, it was one of my chaplains, Father Alberto."

"Thank you." The danger light in his eyes was extinguished, and he picked up his wine cup, drained it, and refilled it. He winced.

"What is the matter?"

"A headache, that is all."

"I am not surprised, given the wine you have put away this evening."

"It is not that. I confess I am all too familiar with those symptoms. I do not know what."

"In any event, I recommend that you stop drinking this evening, take yourself home, and chew willow bark – I have some here for you, look – before retiring."

He smiled, and stood up. "You're a good friend to have, Gerardo." He placed his hands on my shoulders, with an uncomfortable pressure. "Just don't go around listening too much to gossip, that's all I ask." The pressure on my shoulders became a pain as he tightened his grip. "Thank you." He released my shoulders, and smiled, his teeth flashing. "Goodnight."

I blame myself still. Two days after this, Father Alberto's body was found at the bottom of a flight of stone steps, his neck broken.

✝

chapter 27 (Nessuna)

Naturally, 1 had no proof that Pietro was in any way behind this death, but 1 had strong suspicions. 1 knew better than to confront him directly with the deed, though, as 1 knew from past experience what a master of equivocation he was, when he was not actually lying.

I did, however, make my way to the new Prefect, Daniele, to whom I confided some, but not all, of my concerns.

"The steps where Father Anselmo met his death are worn and dangerous," I pointed out. "The Council should appoint someone to mend them before we have another accident." I placed a stress on the last word, which I hoped was subtle.

"Indeed?" the Prefect answered. He turned to the servant behind his chair. "Fetch some refreshment for the Bishop, boy." We were now alone in the room, and Daniele lowered his voice. "I am not as foolish or as ignorant as some would have you believe. But to tell you the truth, I sometimes find myself uttering words that appear to have been put into my mind from outside. Could this be the work of the Devil or one of his demons? I ask myself, and I ask you now."

"May I make a guess?" He nodded. "These utterances come soon after you have talked with the Sub-Prefect?"

"Why, yes, now I come to reflect on the matter. They do."

"I am still puzzled, I confess, but I do not think the Devil is speaking through you. In the meantime…" I changed the subject, observing that the servant was bringing in wine and fruit.

"Ah yes," said the Prefect, seizing his cue, "I will definitely look into that matter of the steps. Shocking business, to be sure."

There was an intelligence under Daniele's mask of foolishness, I concluded. However, his claim about speaking words that were not his concerned me. Somehow, I knew that Pietro was at the bottom of all this, but I could not for the life of me determine how this was so.

As I said, I am compressing events at this point. My time is short – how short, I do not know, but I feel it important that the world should know what took place so many years ago. One further incident before events reach their climax.

Roberto, one of the Guard officers, approached me one morning with a strange tale. On the previous evening, one of his men had sighted Pietro walking along the road to the copse and hollow that I have previously mentioned. This would not be remarkable, since the Sub-Prefect was entitled to leave the city after curfew, but the fact that the gates had not been opened for him was a cause for some concern (I remembered the postern gate to which Pietro possessed the key, but said nothing). The man had obtained permission to follow Pietro at a distance, and proceeded to do so until he reached the hollow.

There, the Guard saw an amazing sight, which he found hard to describe, but according to Fabio, seemed to resemble in some ways the fiery chariot described in the Book of Ezekiel. Shining silver, it had the shape of an upturned platter, some thirty or more cubits across. A bright light shone from underneath it, "as bright as the sun" in Fabio's account. It stood upon four slim pillars that reached to the ground.

As Pietro approached it, a hole appeared in the side of the dish, and steps appeared, that touched the ground. Then in the hole, and walking down the steps, came the angel who had appeared in Vernet's pictures, and whom I had seen talking to Pietro that time. The Guard was terrified, and turned to flee, but before he did so, he saw the angel reach out and take Pietro's hand before leading him up the steps, where he disappeared into the dish. The hole disappeared—

"How can a hole disappear?" I asked Roberto.

"I have no idea," he replied. "I only repeat to you what I was told." He concluded the narrative, telling me that the Guard had started to flee when he heard a strange, almost musical sound, which he could only compare to the sound of a rebec being played by an unskilled performer. Turning, he saw the dish rise from the ground, and terrified, he sank in a swoon. He had no idea how long he lay on the grass, but when he awoke he made his way back to the city, where his fellow Guards informed him that they had seen a bright light arising from that place some time previously.

Roberto, overhearing this excited conversation, had told his men, on pain of severe punishment, not to repeat any of it to any others. "I judged, Your Reverence, that because the Sub-Prefect was involved, it would not be wise to have the story repeated, and given that you are known to be a man of discretion, as well as being a personal friend of the Sub-Prefect's, you might be able to advise us on what we should do. Are we cursed or blessed by this visitation?"

"I know not," I told him, "but one thing is certain. You are not to talk of this with any others. And that applies to all who have heard this story. Allow me to examine the matter, and I will advise you later."

"Thank you, Your Reverence." He bowed and exited.

I never had the chance to advise him. Although the Guard had, according to his officer, clearly and unambiguously witnessed Pietro entering this strange silver dish and ascending to Heaven, the Sub-Prefect was nonetheless seen in the streets in the afternoon of the day on which Roberto made his report. No-one, it seems, had seen him enter the city. Within two days of this, reports were received that a group of bandits were pursuing their evil trade near the city, interrupting trade, and causing the local villagers to be in a state of near-panic. An order went out that a detachment of the City Guards was to investigate and apprehend the bandits. The detachment chosen was composed entirely of those men who had been on duty that strange night, together with their officer, Roberto. We never saw them again. The story had it that they had attacked the bandits, who had fought back with the fury of cornered wolves. No trace of them was ever found, nor were the bandits ever captured.

chapter 28 (Lamakan)

I am writing of the deaths of others. At the time, I was certain that my friend Pietro was at the back of all these events, but I could not be sure, and I was frightened that my knowledge would (as it eventually did) lead to retribution from him.

Now, knowing that the retribution is upon me, I feel at ease. The Imam's words have given me comfort. The journey may be painful, and the departure more so, but the arrival at our goal will be joyous and to be welcomed.

The muezzin calls the faithful to prayer. I pray, but not for myself. I pray for my city, for the friends I have left behind, and for the friends I have here. But to whom do I pray? To the God whom I knew and served faithfully for so many years? To Allah, whose presence here is all-pervasive? Or to Isaac's Adonai, who is older than these? Or are they, as I have come to believe, all different visions of the Ineffable?

☪

chapter 29 (Nessuna)

A little after the disappearance of the guards, I paid a call on Pietro, unannounced. No servant answered the door, and I felt sufficiently at ease to enter the house, given the length and strength of our relationship.

The house appeared to be deserted, but I made my way to the chamber to where Pietro usually did his business. The door was open, and I looked inside.

Pietro was there, but seemingly oblivious to my presence. He was sitting in a chair, his head turned slightly away from me, and his eyes closed. That was perhaps not unexpected. However, what riveted my attention was the headgear that he had donned – the same mysterious skullcap that had been depicted in Vernet's picture of the late Prefect.

As in the picture, the cap was connected to a small box in the shape of a reliquary, studded with gems which appeared to flash in the half-darkness of the room. I observed for some time, and noted that the flashing of the gems seemed to coincide with twitches of Pietro's features, as if he were dreaming, and his dreams were being reflected in the lights emanating from that box.

I decided to say nothing, but quietly crept out of the house, without (as I thought at the time) disturbing him.

It was not long after this that Daniele, the Prefect, began to complain of headaches, which, as he confided to me one day, almost always seemed to coincide with the thoughts that seemed to appear in his head.

"The pain in my head is so intense that I can think of nothing else while it lasts," he complained. "All that I can do is to utter with my mouth the words that invade my mind, and that gives me some relief. But afterwards, I realise that I have been saying things and expressing opinions which are not my own. Indeed, I disagree violently with some of them."

"And do you believe that these views are those of someone in par-ticular? I asked.

"I do," he said.

"No, do not name names," I told him. "I have a good idea of the identity of this person."

"Thank you, Your Reverence. If you could see your way to making this stop...?"

"I cannot make that promise," I said, "as I am unsure of the direction in which I proceed. In the meantime, I will pray for you."

I am afraid that my proposal failed to raise his spirits, and indeed, my prayers seemed to have little effect. It was only three days after my conversation with Daniele that a most extraordinary event took place in the Council meeting. It was one where I was present, since I had been requested to deliver my report in person on the Duomo's prepa-rations for the forthcoming festival.

Pietro was not present, and on my enquiring of my neighbour, an elderly Council member, whether Pietro was often absent from these meetings. It appeared that he was, and on the occasions that he was absent, Daniele's speech often became disordered and disjointed.

"He needs Signor Pietro to guide him," whispered the old man. "His Magnificence is a good enough fellow, but weak, weak."

The meeting was called to order, and Prefect Daniele rose to speak. "Gentlemen and fellow Councillors," he began, and clutched at his forehead. "I feel it is incumbent upon me to speak to you today on the subject of ducks." There was a confused mutter around the table ("Did he say 'ducks'?" "Yes, but why?"). "There are too many of them in this city. We must stamp them out." He sat down abruptly, and put his head in his hands.

Bernardo, who was acting as the Sub-Prefect in Pietro's absence, stood, and attempted to move the subject under discussion to that of the festival, but was continually compelled to yield to the Prefect, who by now seemed obsessed on the subject of ducks, but continued to hold his head, apparently in agony.

I was unable to stand the sight any longer. I rose from my place, and placed my arm around the clearly ailing Prefect's shoulders. "Come, my friend," I said to him. "Come away from this place."

"I cannot," he wailed with a cry that froze my blood. "I must stay here to rid— to rid the city— rid it of ducks." I have never encountered a true case of demonic possession (as I can explain later, this was not demonic possession), but at that time I believed it to be so. I crossed myself, and called for two of the younger Councillors to assist me in taking the poor man from the Council chamber to his home.

Once we had settled Daniele in a chair, I dispatched one of his servants to fetch a physician, who administered a sleeping draught. Almost immediately, his head sank on his chest as he fell into a deep sleep from which he never awakened. The cause of death was unknown, but the physician gave it as his opinion that Daniele's heart was weak, and that the sleeping draught, which would have been an appropriate dose in a healthy man, had exerted a fatal effect on the Prefect in his over-excited condition.

chapter 30 (Nessuna)

Pietro succeeded Daniele as Prefect. He was efficient, I will say that for him, and the standard of life for the ordinary people was improved under his rule.

The streets ceased to be stinking sewers. Fresh wells with clear water were constructed. Beggars disappeared from the streets – many of them were engaged in these public works, and some left the city, never to be seen again (at least, it was assumed that they had left the city – at any event, their faces were no longer a familiar sight).

Families who lacked the resources to buy basic foodstuffs for their families found that the city would provide for them, helping to find jobs, and supplying bread and wine where labour was not to be found.

Need I add that Pietro was liked – no, loved – by the majority of citizens? Never, they said, had there been such a wise and generous Prefect.

It was a different story with the Council and those whom I might term the "nobility" of our city (though we did not, in our city, adopt such titles as Count or Duke). The Council was rarely consulted, and on the rare occasions when it met, Pietro permitted no dissension from his views, which often went against the Councillors' interests. For example, the dole of bread and wine was paid for by a tax on meat. Since the lower classes very seldom ate meat, this was no great hardship on their part, but for persons of rank, for whom meat was a daily household expense, this caused some small anguish.

There were other small nips at their privileges. Without consulting me or any of my clergy, he decreed that there were to be no more reserved places at Mass in the Duomo. The Councillors now found themselves rubbing shoulders, much to their distaste, with those they termed "the great unwashed". To be fair, this was not strictly accurate – the citizens of our city were at least as clean as those of other places I have visited, if not considerably cleaner.

Somehow, though, the mutterings in the Council never seemed to progress beyond being just that – mutterings. Pietro seemed to thrive on his popularity, and the Councillors knew that if they were to make moves against him, they would retain their status as members of the Council no longer, but be pushed from their places by the mob.

To be sure, there were some who talked about the possibility of deposing my friend – if indeed I could still term him such – from his position, but such talk was carried out in whispers, over the winecups, after the servants had cleared away the dishes and platters. It was said that accidents befell those who talked too loudly, and in truth, there had been several incidents which had the appearance of accidents at first sight, but on investigation could easily be taken as the actions of a malign intelligence.

If all was taken into account, it could be said that Pietro had the city where he wanted it – under his thumb. Using the old Roman terms to mark the population, the plebeian element would follow him to the end of the earth, and the patricians were sufficiently cowed not to rebel against his wishes.

chapter 31 (Lamakan)

Ali tells me that the angel is at the gate. It is time.

"Show him in, Ali," I tell him. I compose myself as best as I am able, and recite the Act of Contrition to myself as I wait.

He appears in the doorway from the house to the garden. He is as dazzlingly beautiful as the angels that Vernet painted in another country, seemingly years ago, and whom I saw in that hollow with Pietro. His hair is golden like the sun, and his face shines with the glory of the Lord. As for his garments, they are shining silver. I half-rise to greet him, but he waves a hand, and moves to stand opposite me, looking down at me, unmoving. The heated air is very still. In the distance, a dog barks. Unseen children shout as they tumble and play.

His complexion is flawless – almost like that of a marble statue, and his light blue eyes are fixed on mine. I cannot hold his gaze, and am forced to look away.

He speaks to me, in a voice that thrills me at the same time that it terrifies me.

"I will not hurt you," he tells me. "There will be no pain."

☪

Part VI - Exodus

chapter 32 (Nessuna)

I regarded Pietro – my gaoler who had just described himself as my friend – sitting across the table from me.

"Friends," I agreed. "Of a kind, certainly. I am still the friend of the boy – the young man – with whom I grew up. But am I the friend of the Prefect of this city? Is he my friend?"

Pietro smiled thinly. "We change. Am I the friend of the Bishop? I do not think that I am his friend any more." He drank, and his manner changed as he spoke sharply. "Those notes you made – how much more do you know?"

"Beyond the accidents which are no accident? Beyond those who met Christoforos on a dark night, never to see the sun rise again? Beyond the way you hounded your superiors to gain your present position? Beyond the fact that you have help from the angels? And that you possess a holy relic of some kind?"

Pietro smiled, as one from a great height. "You know it all, and yet you know nothing," he said. "Nothing," he repeated. "And yet, that nothing is dangerous enough. You must not be permitted to tell anyone else of the little you know."

"I can face death," I said. "All I ask is five minutes to commend my soul to the Almighty, and, if possible, that it be a quick clean end."

To my surprise, Pietro laughed. "I could not kill you, Gerardo," he said. "But you must leave the city. I will have you escorted to the nearest port by a company of Guards. Fabio – you are friends, yes? will be in charge of the detachment. I have your word that you will say nothing of tonight's conversation to him, I take it?"

"As long as I have your word that he and his men will continue to live after they have delivered me to the port."

Pietro laughed mirthlessly. "As long as they can keep their mouths shut, they can live. You have my word on it."

"And what will you tell the city?"

"They will be told, because you will write the letter that I am about to dictate to you, that you have taken a sudden fancy to make the pilgrimage to Jerusalem. Indeed, it will be arranged for you that the ship that will meet you at the port will take you to the Holy Land. However, I expect you to go further East, and find a city where you will be able to live at ease, though it will not be a Christian city. I believe there are many such, beyond the Tigris and Euphrates. Naturally, you will not return, and it will be assumed by all here that you have perished in the journey."

Though I had no intention of saying so to Pietro, this plan had some appeal for me. I had previously, as I have mentioned, travelled quite extensively, including countries in which Mohammed is venerated as the Prophet of Allah. The city in which I was born and lived had lost much of the appeal under Pietro that it had possessed when I was younger, and I no longer felt tied to it as I did. "I agree," I said.

"Excellent. You always have been a man of reason, Gerardo. Will you need money?"

"Maybe. I give much of what I have to the poor."

"I know that you do, and it is one of the things for which I admire you. Here." He reached under the table and brought out a leather bag, which he tossed to me. I opened it curiously to discover some stones, and I looked at Pietro curiously.

"Take one out and examine it," he told me.

I did so, and the vivid blue colour alerted me to the treasure he had given to me. "Lapis lazuli," I breathed.

"There is gold under the lapis," Pietro told me. "Gold leaf and ultra-marine for which Vernet had no further use."

"Thank you."

"It is nothing. Now, to your letter."

So, at Pietro's dictation, I wrote that I had been moved by the Holy Spirit to visit the scenes of Our Lord's Passion and Resurrection and to see them with my own eyes. I commended the diocese to my Canons, and expressed my wish that Antonio would be appointed to succeed me as Bishop were I not to return within one year.

"So that is done," Pietro said. "There is one last thing. Stand."

I did so, and Pietro rose also. He moved towards me, threw his arms wide, and embraced me, kissing me full on the lips. I could not help but respond, and the action brought back memories of our boyhood, now worlds away from the men we had become. "I am sorry, Gerardo," he said. "It can be no other way. Some time, perhaps, you may learn what has happened. For now, though, give me your blessing."

He knelt, I gave him my benediction and signed him with the sign of the cross.

"And now," he said, rising, and summoning Fabio. "Farewell."

He turned away, and I never saw his face again.

I am relieved a little by the angel's words. I invite him to come and sit with me under the date palm, and call Ali over to us. "May I offer you some refreshment?" I ask him. "Some sherbet, a few dates, some almonds or pistachios, perhaps?" The laws of hospitality are not to be broken, even when one's guest is also probably one's murderer.

He smiles, thinly. "You are a most generous host, but I must decline your hospitality. Such things are not for me."

"You do not mind if I eat or drink in your presence? This is not a religious objection, I take it?"

"Oh, by all means go ahead. I perceive that this will make our conversation easier for you."

I request Ali to fetch my drink and fruit, and settle myself as comfortably as I am able. "May I know your name, sir?" I ask him.

Again that thin smile. "It would mean nothing to you. You may call me Azrael if you like."

"So you are indeed an angel? The angel of death?"

Azrael shakes his head. "No. I am a mortal being, like yourself. If no accidents befall me, I will live for many times longer than one of your kind, however. I am presently," he pauses for a moment, "between six and seven thousand of your years old. However, much of that time has been spent in sleep."

"And your home city? You are from the North? The land of ice and snow, and winters of perpetual night?"

"My country is not of this world," he smiles. "But it is not Heaven as you understand it."

I no longer understand what I mean by Heaven. Is it the paradise as promised by the Prophet (peace be upon him), a garden of pleasure, or the celestial city described by Saint John in his terrible vision of the End of Days? Or, as Isaac has hinted, a mystical union with the Almighty?

"Hell, then?" I suggest. "Though you say are mortal, are you indeed," and I cross myself reflexively, "what we might call a demon?"

He does not flinch. "Some have termed us so. Also, some have termed us angels. Again, we are like you. We are caught between Heaven and Hell."

"Then there is a Heaven and also a Hell?"

"Oh, assuredly."

"So you are a Christian?" He shakes his head. "A Jew? A Muslim?"

"No, no, and no. I follow no religion that is of this world."

I sit and sip the cool drink that Ali has just placed before me. "You tell me that your city and your religion is not of this world. And yet you tell me that you are not from Heaven or from Hell. Where is your world?"

He says nothing, but points upwards. "But I repeat," he reminds me, "that it is not Heaven."

I am puzzled. "You are from the Moon, perhaps? Or the Sun?"

His smile seems more genuine this time. "Oh, my friend, you have no conception. Out there, beyond the blue sky, lies an infinite expanse of empty blackness. A vast sea of emptiness, with tiny motes of luminous dust floating in it. And those motes, we call suns. That up there," and he points to the Sun, "is just one of those motes."

"There are other suns, circling other worlds?"

"It is actually the other way round. An infinite number of worlds circle an infinite number of suns, but whether it is that or the other is not really important. Believe me when I tell you that there are more worlds and more suns, which you see as stars, than there are grains of sand in the desert that surrounds this city."

He pauses, and my mind begins to take in the immensity of what he is telling me.

"And they are a long way away?"

"Further than you can imagine. Let us imagine, for example, that these two pebbles here, with a hair's breadth separating them, represent this city and Rome. This hair's breadth is the distance between the two cities. If we were to shrink the distance between here and the Sun to the same scale, the Sun would be the same distance as in Rome from here in reality."

My head swims. I can hardly begin to comprehend the scale of what he is describing. "And between here and the Sun, there is what?" I croak out at last.

"Nothing. No air, almost no light, and no solid matter, other than a few rocks."

"But you travelled all that distance?"

"We travelled many times further than that. Can you now understand the distance to the Sun?"

I nod. "I think so," I say, but my mind is still staggering with the vast distances involved.

"Good." He smiles. "Now look at these two pebbles again. The distance between them is now the distance between the Earth and the Sun. The Sun of my home, which you call a star in Capricorn, is three times further than the distance between here and Rome."

I sway on my seat, and I believe I am going to fall. The world swims before my eyes as I slowly comprehend the staggering distance this must be from us.

"How do you travel such distances?"

"We sleep. I told you, did I not, that I was many thousands of years old, but I slept for many of them. It is a deep sleep. We do not dream. We know nothing of time passing."

I cross myself. "You are magicians. I have heard stories of magicians and kings, asleep until their people call for them."

"It is not magic, merely the application of natural philosophy."

My mind is still full of wonder. I have only just begun to appreciate the distances that separate our world from those tiny dots of light that shine above the desert at night. Now I must come to terms with the idea that Adam and Eve were not the first of God's creation to acknowledge Him, but these angelic beings, many hundreds of thousands of thousands of leagues from us, were witnesses to His glory, and perhaps even knew and worshipped Him in a time before there was Man. I am bursting with questions to which I must know the answers.

"Ask them," he says.

"Are you aware of my thoughts?" I ask him.

"Yes," he says without hesitation. "But there is no magic in it. Simply a gift that my people have. Your people have a gift that I personally envy – that of making music. The concept had never occurred to any of us before. It is an enviable gift."

"How many of you are there here now?" I ask.

"Seven," he tells me. "Seven arrived here some hundred years ago. On my home world, several million of us, in a thousand cities."

"And where are you seven living here?"

"In many places. We move from place to place. However, we often return to our larger ship which sails between the stars and brought us here, and is now circling the earth. We use smaller craft for this purpose."

I ask the most important question of all. "And were you created by God?"

"We believe so." He says no more, and I feel he is holding something back. Now is not the time to ask more, but I feel a sense of God's greatness. If what he says is true (and it is so improbable that I cannot help but believe it, for who would create such an elaborate falsehood?), then God is truly everywhere, and the whole of Creation is so much more than Holy Church, or the Prophet (peace be upon him), or Isaac's Torah and Talmud tell us. My mind falls spinning into this empty space between the worlds he has described. And yet it is not empty, because I have the perfect faith that God is the God of the spaces between the suns, just as much as he is the God of our world, and all that is in it.

I remain silent, but recite the Te Deum to myself in my head. Allahu Akbar - as my friend the Imam would say. God is great. How much greater than he or I ever imagined. Adonai – the Lord of Hosts – as Isaac would have Him. But how many more hosts and a greater lord than Isaac knows. And my Lord, the Almighty and Eternal God – almighty and omnipotent and omnipresent in a way that I could never have imagined. I can die happy, now that I have caught a glimpse of the true greatness of God.

I lean back in my seat, overcome, and I realise that there is a smile on my face.

Azrael sees my expression, and smiles back. There is no cruelty in it. He seems to see my happiness at the realisation of the immensity of God.

"How many times...?" I ask, after a few minutes of silence.

"Has He come to visit His creation, as your Jesus did to you?" Azrael completes my sentence for me. "I cannot tell you. We have not been so blessed, but we have had a Messenger from Him, similar to your Mohammed. However, I personally know of two other worlds where God has revealed Himself to His creatures directly."

"Praise be to Him, who loves His Creation," I murmur to myself, and am surprised when Azrael adds his "Amen".

"No, do not be surprised," he tells me. "Rather, it is I who am surprised by you."

☪

chapter 34 (Lamakan)

Azrael's words take me aback.

"You are surprised by me?" I enquire incredulously. "You tell me you are from another world, an uncountable distance from here, that you are thousands of years old, and, more importantly, that God is present throughout all the worlds, and you are the one who is surprised?"

"I am," he tells me. "When you lived in the same city as Pietro, I had marked you down as yet another of those priests who lived only in their own tiny circle of belief. Now I see that you are open to so much more than many of your colleagues."

"You know Pietro, then?" My mind is struggling to put together the pieces of this puzzle, even though I believed I had assembled it in my head some years ago.

"Of course. My sister was, after all, the model for that painter's angels."

"Your sister?"

"We seven are a family. It was my sister whom Pietro encountered first. 'Sister' is perhaps a simplification of her relationship to me, but the term will serve us for now. She took a liking to him. Despite the slight differences between our races, attraction can make itself apparent."

"' 'The Nephilim were on the earth in those days, and also afterward, when the sons of God came in to the daughters of man and they bore children to them. These were the mighty men who were of old, the men of renown,'" I murmur to myself, remembering the words of the sixth chapter of the Book of Genesis.

"Indeed so. Though those that you call the 'sons of God' in your book were of a different race to us, they must have been similar – visitors from a far-off sun – perhaps more closely resembling your race than do we, hence permitting some intimacy, which would not be possible in our case. Despite a more than superficial resemblance, we are composed of different stuff. But attraction and even affection between individuals, as I say, can transcend boundaries. In this case, it was one of your men who caught the eye of one of our females. He was singing to himself, and as I say, music is an attractive novelty to us."

"Pietro?"

"Indeed."

"How did he first encounter her?"

"She was descending from our starship in one of our smaller sky-craft. She believed herself to have landed in a deserted area near your city. Pietro was there – for what purpose, she knew not."

"Probably he was expecting to meet some peasant girl with whom he had formed relations."

"Maybe, though at that time he himself was a youth, little more than a young boy. In any event, he received more than he expected, in the form of my sister's gratitude. In return for the pleasure that he gave her with his singing, she presented him with a toy which allowed him to control, to some extent, the thoughts and actions of those around him. She perceived that he already possessed some considerable ability in that direction, and felt it was an appropriate gift, though he was perhaps too young, and in my opinion, not of a suitable temperament to be presented with such a toy."

"A toy that resembles a skullcap, attached by a cord to a small box resembling a reliquary?"

He starts in surprise. "You know of it? Pietro let you see it?"

"Not intentionally, and he never explained its purpose. But did you know that it was on show as part of a picture by the painter Vernet? It was shown on a table by the then Prefect of the city. Your sister was in that painting, as an angel."

"I knew that she had been depicted in at least one painting," he tells me. "Your race's skills in this, as in music, are a marvel to us. We have much to learn from you. But I had no idea that the fool Pietro had exposed us in this way."

"And she continued to meet him?"

"The toy needs power, energy, call it what you will, which is provided by a small source. This source is not infinite, and must be replaced."

"What is its appearance?"

"A small silver object, about the size of one of your thumbs."

From inside my robe, I bring the small silver cylinder that I had picked up from the field so long ago and have kept with me ever since. Azrael looks at me in astonishment.

"Where did you find that?" he asks, taking it from me.

"From the place where your sister met Pietro."

He laughs. "She was always careless. We were all angry with her for her forming this attachment to Pietro, and for her gift of the thought-projector to him. It was not in our interest to be so visible. Nor, as I say, did we consider it appropriate."

I consider the angel's words (I cannot think of him as anything other than the angel I took him for at first). Now it is clear to me how Pietro was able to manipulate and use others in his climb to the Prefecture, and how he was able to control the city and the Council so easily.

"You wished to remain hidden? But why have you shown yourself so openly here in this city?"

"There are times when boldness will conquer all. My display in the market was intended to promote awe and not a little fear."

"It succeeded in that aim," I tell him. "At least, as far as some of my acquaintance are concerned."

"But you should know," he tells me, "that we are not here as your enemies. We are here to study you. Your music and your painting fascinate us."

"But you are now here to kill me," I objected. "I am ready."

Azrael looks at me curiously. "Why should I kill you?"

"Because I know all about you. I know the secrets you have just told me. I know how Pietro has won his position through the help of those who are not human – whom many would see as demons and instruments of evil. I have too much knowledge."

He laughs. "Why should any of that matter, now that Pietro is dead?"

"Dead?" I cross myself.

"The mob tore him to pieces. He had promised bread and wine to all, and there was none after ten days. The merchants refused to sell him any more, and the Guards refused to threaten the merchants to force them to give up their provisions. He died quickly, if it is any comfort to you," he adds, seeing my distress at the news of the death of my friend.

"And now?" I ask, when I have composed myself a little.

"We are departing this world. I came to tell you that should you wish to return to your city, you may do so."

I consider the vast distances, the infinity of suns, and the presence of God there. "Take me with you to your sun," I ask, hardly knowing what I am saying.

Azrael shakes his head. "You cannot. Our world is not… is not like yours. You could not live there. I am sorry. I know you would be one of the few we have seen here who would appreciate it, but believe me, it is not possible. Return to your city."

It is my turn to shake my head. "No. I am too old. And I have friends here. Friends who, like you, help me understand the greatness of God."

"Then rest here, my friend, and live in the greatness of God." He stands, and passes the small cylinder back to me. "Keep this. A gift from thousands of years, and millions of leagues. Remember us, and pray for us."

"I will."

I watch my silver-clad visitor depart. Ali and Fatima are watching, terrified, from one of the windows of the house, but Azrael appears not to notice them. And then he is gone.

I sink back in my seat and close my eyes. My reverie is broken by Ali's voice. I have no idea exactly how long I was travelling between the stars in my mind, but when I open my eyes, the sun has moved a considerable distance in the sky.

I am alive. I am not dead, and I am not about to be killed. I know I should be relieved by this, but to tell the truth, it does not seem to be of great significance. I have learned great truths, which are more important than the mere matter of my death. I sigh deeply, knowing that I will never again approach this depth of understanding while I am alive.

"Are you well?" Ali asks, with concern. "Will you be leaving us? What did he want? Was he a djinn or an angel?"

"Too many questions, my friend. Yes, no, nothing, no." I smile. "Ali, invite Isaac ben Yeshua and the Imam tonight to join us all in the house for a great feast. Let us celebrate the greatness of God together."

Other books by Hugh Ashton

Tales from the Deed Box of John H. Watson M.D.
More from the Deed Box of John H. Watson M.D.
Secrets from the Deed Box of John H. Watson M.D.
The Darlington Substitution
The Trepoff Murder
The Bradfield Push
Notes from the Dispatch-Box of John H. Watson M.D.
Further Notes from the Dispatch-Box of John H. Watson M.D.
The Reigate Poisoning Case: Concluded
The Death of Cardinal Tosca
Without my Boswell
The Last Notes from the Dispatch-Box of John H. Watson M.D.
1894
Some Singular Cases of Mr. Sherlock Holmes
The Lichfield Murder
The Deed Box of John H. Watson M.D.
The Dispatch-box of John H. Watson M.D.

Beneath Gray Skies
Red Wheels Turning
Tales of Old Japanese
At the Sharpe End
The Untime
The Untime Revisited
Leo's Luck
Balance of Powers

Sherlock Ferret and the Missing Necklace
Sherlock Ferret and the Multiplying Masterpieces
Sherlock Ferret and the Poisoned Pond
Sherlock Ferret and the Phantom Photographer
The Adventures of Sherlock Ferret

The Author

Hugh Ashton was born in the United Kingdom, and moved to Japan in 1988, where he lived until a return to the UK in 2016. He is best known for his Sherlock Holmes stories, which have been hailed as some of the most authentic pastiches on the market, and have received favourable reviews from Sherlockians and non-Sherlockians alike.

He currently divides his time between the historic cities of Lichfield, and Kamakura, a little to the south of Yokohama, with his wife, Yoshiko.

More about Hugh Ashton and his books may be found at:
http://HughAshtonBooks.info
and he may be contacted at:

HAshton@mac.com

9 781912 605118